O9-AIC-533

THE SKELETON IN THE CLOSET

PREVIOUS MYSTERIES BY M. C. BEATON

Agatha Raisin

Agatha Raisin and the Fairies of Fryfam
Agatha Raisin and the Witch of Wyckhadden
Agatha Raisin and the Wizard of Evesham
Agatha Raisin and the Wellspring of Death
Agatha Raisin and the Terrible Tourist
Agatha Raisin and the Murderous Marriage
Agatha Raisin and the Walkers of Dembley
Agatha Raisin and the Potted Gardener
Agatha Raisin and the Vicious Vet
Agatha Raisin and the Quiche of Death

Hamish Macbeth

Death of an Addict
Death of a Scriptwriter
Death of a Dentist
Death of a Macho Man
Death of a Nag
Death of a Charming Man
Death of a Travelling Man
Death of a Glutton
Death of a Prankster
Death of a Snob
Death of a Hussy
Death of a Perfect Wife
Death of an Outsider
Death of a Cad
Death of a Gossip

THE SKELETON IN THE CLOSET

†

M. C. BEATON

ST. MARTIN'S MINOTAUR
NEW YORK

All characters in this book, including the town of Buss, are fictional.

 For information, address St. Martin's Press, 175 Fifth Avenue, New York, N.Y. 10010.

www.minotaurbooks.com

ISBN 0-312-20772-7

First Edition: March 2001

10 9 8 7 6 5 4 3 2 1

For Chris and Stella Jury
And their children, Maisie and Joseph
~With affection~

ONE

†

IN the way that illiterate people become very cunning at covering up their disability, Mr. Fellworth Dolphin, known as Fell, approaching forty, was still a virgin and kept it a dark secret.

His long-standing virginity had come about because he had been a shy, lanky, oversensitive boy, the single child of strict and emotionally blackmailing parents. He had been born when his mother was in her early forties. His father, a railway signalman, and his mother, a housewife, had dinned it into him that his duty in life was to get an education and be the sole support of his parents. When he was older, they chose "suitable" girls for him, girls who seemed foreign to the young Fell with their vapid conversation and the way their minds seemed to be set on a white wedding and a neat bungalow, both with a total absence of romance. For Fell was a romantic, living through books.

He had been set to go to university, but his father had fallen ill and it was borne in on him that he must take some sort of job immediately or "they would all starve." They lived in the market town of Buss in Worcestershire. In Buss, there was a rather grand hotel, the Palace, and it was there that young Fell found employment as a waiter.

His father died from a heart attack several years after Fell had started work. His mother became cross and morose, always complaining. Sometimes when he had finished a late shift in the hotel dining room, he would return home to their scrupulously clean two-up two-down terraced house, and he would see the light in the living room still burning and his feet would feel as heavy as lead for he knew he would have to drink the hot milk he hated and listen to his mother's complaints. In his spare time, he lived through books: spy books, adventure books, detective stories, thrillers, relishing those other worlds of action and mayhem.

He had acquaintances, but no close friends.

Although he was not often prone to depression, as he approached his thirty-eighth birthday, and once more walked home from the hotel, he felt a terrible darkness of the soul. Life had passed him by. He did not look unpleasing, being tall with a good figure, a pleasant face with wide-spaced grey eyes and a long, sensitive mouth. But his thick hair had turned prematurely grey.

The light was on in the living room. He braced himself for another wearying end to the day, listening to his mother's droning complaints, cradling that glass of hot milk and wondering if he could tip it somewhere.

He had not been allowed his own key. "Why should you have one?" his mother had complained. "I'm always here." But he had secretly had one cut, just a little bit of rebellion. He rang the bell. Nothing. The door did not open, nor did his mother's whiskery face appear at the window.

He took out his key and let himself in. He went into the living room. His mother was lying back in her usual armchair. He knew somehow that she was dead.

He felt numb. He phoned the ambulance and the police. He travelled in the ambulance to the hospital. He was told in hushed whispers that she, like his father, had suffered a heart attack.

He walked home at dawn—he had never been allowed to take driving lessons—trying to fight down a guilty feeling of relief. He was free at last from the chains of duty.

As he plodded homeward, he looked about him at the silent streets of the market town. This town had been his cell. He had never even been to London. The clock on the town hall sent down six silvery chimes. The rising sun sent his elongated shadow stretching out in front of him. He shivered, although the day was already warm. What on earth was going to become of him?

The next day a call from Mr. Jamieson, one of the town's solicitors, came as a surprise. Mr. Jamieson said a doctor friend at the hospital had told him of Mrs. Dolphin's death, and asked Fell to call round at his office to go through his mother's will. Fell could not imagine how his mother, who never seemed to leave the house, had got round to writing a will and visiting a lawyer. Fell had already phoned the hotel to say he would be taking time off until after the funeral. He still felt strangely numb. He put on his only suit and a shirt which his mother had turned at the collar and cuffs when they became frayed, a dark blue tie and highly polished shoes. He could now let his shoes get dirty if he liked, he thought, and then was ashamed at the pettiness of the thought. As he clattered down the stairs to make his way out, he looked at his mother's usual chair by the window, almost amazed to see it empty.

Mr. Jamieson seemed too young to have had any dealings with Fell's mother. He appeared to be in his early thirties. He had thick, shiny black hair and a smooth face with pale eyes behind horn-rimmed glasses. After commiserating with Fell on his mother's sudden death, he got down to business. "Your father," said Mr. Jamieson, "left everything to your mother on his death and Mrs. Dolphin left everything to you."

"It won't be much," said Fell apologetically, for the lawyer's offices seemed too grand to deal with such a small inheritance, "although I suppose I will get the house."

"It is in fact a very comfortable amount of money."

Fell blinked at him. It was a sunny day. The weekly market in the town square below the windows was in full swing. The sun glittered on the glass front of a large bookcase.

The lawyer smiled. "Did you never look at your parents' bank books?"

Fell gave a rueful smile. "I haven't had time to look through any bank books or documents."

"Well, apart from the house, there is the sum of five hundred thousand pounds, plus some shares. Of course, there will be death duties to pay. The first two hundred and fifty thousand is tax-free, and then there is a straight forty per cent off the remainder."

"But that's impossible!" Fell turned red. "Quite impossible. We never even had a television set."

"Your father saved as much as he could all his life. The savings were kept in a high-interest account."

"But I couldn't go to university! I had to go to work. They lived on my earnings!"

"Perhaps they wanted to make sure you had a comfortable future."

It burst out of Fell. "But they took my youth."

The lawyer looked uncomfortable. "To business, Mr. Dolphin. I have been made an executor. Would you like me to arrange the funeral?"

"Please," said Fell, still bewildered and shaken. "I wouldn't know where to start."

"The expenses from the funeral will be paid out of the estate. These things take some time to wind up, but in the meantime you can draw any money in advance."

"May I draw, say, two thousand pounds now?" Fell did not know how he had the temerity to ask for such a sum.

"Certainly."

When Fell left the lawyer's office, he could feel rage boiling up inside him. He was free at last—free to travel, to set up his own business, to start living. But his parents had filleted out his ambition and his guts. He felt like someone who has come out of prison after a long sentence, wondering how to cope with life and reality and the modern world.

He did not even have a bank account. He had handed his pay cheques first to his father, and then, after his father's death, to his mother, and a small sum had been handed back to him.

He went into the nearest bank, holding the lawyer's cheque, and opened an account. It was all so easy.

Then he returned home and began to go through his father's

old desk. Tucked away in a drawer at the bottom was a cash box. It was locked. With a strange feeling of intrusion, he searched his mother's battered old calfskin handbag. On her ring of keys was a little silver one. He inserted it in the lock and found it worked. He opened the box up. It was full of money in neat bundles, each marked "one thousand pounds." With shaking fingers, he counted it out. There was nearly fifty thousand pounds. He was about to put it back in the box, take it round to the bank and put it in his new account when he suddenly began to wonder how his father had come by such a large amount of loose cash. He had obviously not declared it to the income tax.

Fell went to the sideboard and took out a bottle of whisky which had been produced only at Christmas and poured himself a generous measure. He sat sipping it, looking around the living room, at the dark cheap furniture, at the old horsehair—horsehair!—sofa and the brown paint on the doors and skirting and the dull, faded wallpaper. He felt trapped in these familiar surroundings. What did his inheritance matter? He would never have the courage to do anything with it. He roused himself to find the address book which held the numbers of the few surviving relatives and phoned them, telling them he would let them know the day and time of the funeral. Then the undertaker's rang. Fell agreed on the price of a coffin, and that the body should be buried in the town cemetery in three days' time at ten in the morning. The undertaker asked if Mrs. Dolphin had been Jewish, Catholic or Protestant. Fell told him, "Church of England," and the efficient undertaker said he would contact the vicar of St. Peter's to conduct the service. Fell replaced the receiver. He suddenly wanted his mother back, so that he could ask her why they had skimped and saved all those years. He wanted to ask her what she had thought about during her long days in the house alone. But it was now too late.

He rang the relatives again and informed them of the time of the funeral and the date. Things like that he could do. He had always been dutiful.

The next day, the doorbell rang and he went to answer it. The ancient and unlovely figure of his mother's sister, Aunt Agnes, stood on the doorstep.

"Come in, Aunt," said Fell. "Have you come all the way down from Wales?"

"Yes, but I'm staying with my friend, Nancy, in Worcester until after the funeral." Her eyes ranged round the living room. "There are some nice pieces here. You'll need someone to look after you. Doris always said"—Doris was the late Mrs. Dolphin—" 'I don't know who's going to take care of my boy when I'm gone and give him his hot milk.' So I've decided to sacrifice myself. I'll move in with you."

Terror gripped Fell. His aunt looked remarkably like his late mother. Whiskery face, small weak eyes, round figure in a tightly buttoned jacket.

"How kind of you," he said. "But I am surprised my mother didn't tell you. I'm engaged. This tragic business, of course, puts off the wedding."

Aunt Agnes sat down suddenly and goggled at him. "Who is she?"

Desperation lending his fantasy wings, Fell said, "Maggie Partlett."

There was a waitress at the hotel in which he worked called Maggie Partlett. She was extremely plain with thick glasses, lank hair and a lumpy figure.

"What does she do?"

"She works as a waitress, same hotel as me."

"Well, I never. And you've got the house and all this lovely furniture."

It seemed as if something had broken loose in Fell. "Maggie doesn't like the stuff," he said. "Tell you what, after the funeral, I'll put it all in a delivery van and send it up to you in Wales."

Aunt Agnes said, "That's awfully good of you. All this lovely stuff. I 'member when they bought it. Oh, my. You *are* a good boy. And that's what I'll tell this Maggie of yours when I meet her at the funeral."

"She won't be there. Her mother in Bedford isn't well, so she's over there at the moment."

"Sad. But I'll come back in a few months and you can introduce me then. I must be on my way."

"Let me get you a taxi and pay for it."

"What! All the way to Worcester."

"I've got a bit saved up."

"I must say, it would be better than waiting in this heat for a bus. It's going to be a scorcher of a summer. It's the dandelions, you see."

"Dandelions?"

"Yes, dandelions. You'll have seen masses of them all along the roads on the verges. Country people always said when you saw a lot of dandelions, it was going to be a hot summer."

"Dandelion summer," said Fell and laughed.

"You must forgive me laughing," he said quickly. "Grief takes me that way." And God forgive me, he said silently to himself, because I am not grieving at all.

†

When his aunt had left, he wondered why he had not told her about the legacy. Most of his other relatives were dead. But there was Cousin Barbara, and Cousin Tom. He should maybe see the lawyer and share it out. No, cried a voice in his head. I earned it with every bit of my youth. It was then he began to cry because he had not loved his mother and he was glad she was dead.

After some time, he dried his eyes and began to look through his home with new eyes. There were two bedrooms upstairs, a living room and sitting room downstairs and a small kitchen. The sitting room was kept for "best," in the old country way: three-piece suite with the plastic covers still over the uncut moquette upholstery, a fringed standard lamp, the shade covered in plastic, a display cabinet with bits of china, a fitted mushroom carpet, and a glass coffee table on white wrought-iron legs. He mentally cleared it all out and stripped the heavy flock wallpaper from the walls, tore up the carpet to find what was underneath. What if, once he had cleared everything out—just what if he turned the living room into a large kitchen, with modern appliances, with long counters, shiny copper pans and bunches of herbs? His eyes filled with tears of guilt again. Something dark was telling him that his days of living would never come. Better leave things as they were. Go home every night to the dark, lonely house and hear the ghost of his mother's complaining voice.

He had to get out again, into the sunlight, take action, any action. He walked to a driving school and booked in for a course of lessons, he ordered a television set to be delivered that very day, then he went to the hotel and handed in his notice.

He was just leaving the hotel when with a guilty start he saw Maggie arriving for the evening shift.

"Oh, Fell," she said, blinking at him through her thick glasses, "I am so very sorry about your mother."

"Thank you, Maggie. I've resigned."

"It won't be the same place without you," she said shyly. They were both book readers and talked a lot about their favourite authors.

"Look here, Maggie, I did a silly thing. My aunt was threatening to move in with me and I told a lie on the spur of the moment. I said I was engaged to you."

If I were pretty, you wouldn't find it so silly, thought Maggie. Aloud she said, "What will you do when she finds out it isn't true?"

"I'll cope with that later," said Fell, suddenly weary.

"I don't mind pretending," said Maggie quickly. "I mean, we could always break it off after the funeral."

Fell looked down at her as if seeing her for the first time. Her lank hair could do with cutting and shaping, and her clothes were a ragbag of shapelessness, and the thick glasses were ugly, but her mouth was well shaped and her eyes were kind.

"That's good of you," he said.

"Do you want me to go to the funeral?"

Fell laughed and Maggie blinked up at him, thinking that she had never heard Fell laugh before. "I told Auntie that you were nursing your sick mother in Bedford."

"I think you'll need some support at the funeral," said Maggie practically. "You'll need to have some drinks and eats for them at the house."

"I didn't think of that."

"You can tell Auntie she misheard. My mother is home in bed, not Bedford. I think she'd buy that one and then you can leave the catering to me. It can be expensive."

"As far as expense is concerned, Maggie, I think maybe we'd better meet for lunch tomorrow if you're free. I've got something to tell you I don't want anyone to know."

"I'd love that. Where?"

"That French restaurant down by the river—at one o'clock?"

"All right. I'll pay my share."

"That's what I want to talk to you about. I'll pay. But don't tell anyone."

"That's not hard," said Maggie ruefully. "No one talks to me except that wretched Italian barman who's always jeering at me."

"I'll see you then."

Fell headed home, just in time to see the television van arriving. What, he wondered guiltily, would the elderly neighbours on either side make of an aerial being erected on the roof and a television set being carried indoors right after his mother's death? He felt suddenly ashamed, but he had used up his small stock of courage for the day and somehow could not tell the television men he had changed his mind.

He tipped the men, and when they had left, decided to watch something on television.

A ring at the doorbell.

He jumped guiltily and somehow his thoughts immediately flew to the money in the cash box, now diminished by a wad of notes in his wallet.

He opened the door. The vicar, Mr. Sneddon, stood on the step.

His heart sank. He did not like Mr. Sneddon, for Mr. Sneddon was unoriginal. He had read about Mr. Sneddon in many books, the trendy clap-happy vicar with a burning desire to attract the spotty youth of Buss to the church while disaffecting all his regulars. It is all very irritating when a character who has been written to death turns up on one's doorstep.

Mr. and Mrs. Dolphin had been regular attenders while the old vicar had been in office, but Mrs. Dolphin had latterly given up going to church, sitting behind the lace curtains in the living room watching the world go by.

"Come in," said Fell, thinking, no lace curtains ever again.

The vicar came in and sat down. He was wearing a scarlet shell suit and trainers. He had very big feet. People with very big feet should not wear trainers, thought Fell, because those feet dominated the small room.

"My boy," began the vicar, who was about the same age as Fell, "this is a dark day for you."

"Indeed," murmured Fell.

"I gather the undertakers, Taylor and Fenwick, have all the arrangements?"

"Yes, the lawyer is kindly attending to everything."

"I will gladly officiate. Are there any special hymns you would like?"

"I would like 'To Be a Pilgrim,' the Twenty-third Psalm, and 'Onward Christian Soldiers.' "

The vicar frowned. "I feel that 'Onward Christian Soldiers' is a teensy bit militant."

Fell was about to back down, but suddenly found himself saying calmly, "Those are the hymns Mother would have wanted. And the burial service from the old Book of Common Prayer."

"But we must move with the times and—"

"The old Book of Common Prayer. I—I mean Mother—preferred it."

"Very well," said the vicar reluctantly.

After the vicar had left, Fell suddenly wanted to get out of the house. He decided to go for a walk. The river Buss bisected the town, flowing between the old castle gardens. Buss Castle had been a second home in medieval times of one of the Earls of Warwick. It was now owned by the National Trust. Its thick walls plunged straight down into the glassy waters of the river, where launches and barges ploughed up and down and willow trees trailed their new leaves in the water.

The castle gardens were almost deserted. Fell sat down on a bench by the river as two swans cruised past. I'm like that, thought Fell. Serene on the top and the little paddles of my brain working furiously underneath. Why all that cash?

His parents had surely been law-abiding—strictly so. His father had always been complaining about layabouts and drug takers. Why not put the money in the bank? Had it been hidden from the tax man? But why? If it had been legally come by . . .

His busy thoughts turned to Maggie. It would be nice to have a confidante. Maggie was kind and trustworthy. Fell was not nervous in her presence, because he did not see her as a woman. In his many fantasies, women were always tall and beautiful and long-legged. Perhaps he might have asked a woman out in the past, but that would have meant asking his parents for the money to entertain her and then facing endless questions. And the fact was that both his dumpy little parents had possessed very powerful and domineering personalities. His father had given up beating him when he was twelve, but Fell could still remember the terror he had experienced when his mother would utter those dreaded words, "Your father will deal with you when he gets home." Then the waiting to endure the beating on the bare backside with his father's leather belt. He had never spoken to anyone about those beatings and had assumed for a long time after they had stopped that they were all part of parenting.

He rose and walked up the main street. So many shops containing so many things he could now buy if he wanted. He stood outside a men's outfitter's and then stared at his dim reflection in the shop window. His suit was shabby and the material cheap.

Again he thought of the money. He should really share it with the few relatives he had. But he would put it off until the funeral.

He bought himself fish and chips, went home and switched on the television set and lost himself in the moving coloured pictures until midnight.

He rose early next morning and with a new feeling of adventure went to the local Marks & Spencer and bought a blazer, trousers, striped shirt and silk tie. Then he went to the jeweller's. He would need to buy a ring for Maggie. At first as he looked at the engagement rings, he thought that anything simple might do. But at last he shook his head and refused them all. Maggie was doing him a great favour. Why not buy her a ring that she could keep, something more original?

He went into an antique shop where he knew they had a case of jewellery. With great care he finally selected a Victorian heavy gold ring, with a large square-cut emerald. The price made his eyelids blink rapidly. He paid cash, but with a dark little worm of doubt again plaguing his brain. Where had the money come from? He banished the thought and retired home and changed into his new clothes. He was beginning to feel like a totally different person.

Maggie was nervously waiting outside the striped awning of the restaurant, which was in an old Georgian mansion beside the river in the castle gardens. Fell would never know what pains Maggie had gone to with her appearance. She was wearing a long biscuit-coloured linen skirt, a tailored jacket and a lemon silk blouse. Fell only saw reassuringly familiar Maggie.

They went into the restaurant. The restaurant, although very grand, did not intimidate Fell. He was armoured in his new clothes. He had left shabby Fell behind.

They were given a table by the French windows which opened onto the terrace.

"You order for me," whispered Maggie. "I eat anything."

Fell ordered a simple meal of cucumber soup, followed by poached salmon and salad, and then with great daring also ordered a bottle of champagne. When the waiter had gone off with his order, he produced the jeweller's box and handed it to Maggie. "It's for you," he said. "You may as well look the part."

Maggie opened the box. The emerald blazed up at her. She caught her breath. She was suddenly intensely aware of everything, of the sunlight sparkling off the cutlery, of the peppery smell of the geraniums in pots on the terrace, of the chuckling sound of the river.

"It's beautiful," she said. "Is it real?"

"I hope so."

"I'll give it back to you."

"No, don't do that. I wanted to give you something special, something you could keep."

Maggie gave a shaky laugh. "It matches my eyes."

Fell looked at her, puzzled.

"See?" She removed her heavy glasses. Her eyes were very large and green with flecks of gold.

"You have beautiful eyes," said Fell. "You should wear contact lenses."

Those eyes filled with tears. "What's the matter?" asked Fell quickly.

Maggie took out a handkerchief and dried her eyes and put her glasses firmly back on. "I'm just tired, Fell, that's all. You know what it's like. The last customers didn't leave until one in the morning. Now, first I had to tell my mother about our engagement. She doesn't know it's a pretend engagement and wants to meet you. I told her you were too grief-stricken, and then afterwards I can tell her it's all off."

"I hate making you lie for me."

"I always lie to my mother anyway. It's a form of self-protection. My father's dead. Mother always says I'll never get a man, so from time to time I invent a boyfriend. They never jilt me, you know, they either die or go abroad. Anyway, enough about me. What do you want to talk to me about?"

Fell had meant to tell her only about the inheritance. But somehow, under her sympathetic eyes, he found himself beginning at the beginning. He told her everything—about his childhood, about his relief at his mother's death, about his guilt, and about the mysterious money in the cash box. He ended by saying, "I can't understand why I didn't tell the relatives about the money I'd been left or offer to give them some. I don't know their financial circumstances. My parents never talked about them. They never really talked much about anything. I only know I want all the money for myself. Is that greedy?"

"No, it's your inheritance. You'll never satisfy them. You'll simply cause a lot of envy and upset. We'll talk to them at the funeral and find out if any of them need money. If they don't, you've got nothing to worry about. It's yours, so keep it."

"I'm worried about that fifty thousand. I've already started to make a hole in it."

"I can't believe it's anything illegal. Was there anything else in the desk to give you a clue?"

"I didn't look further."

"I'll come back with you after lunch. I took the day off. I'll need to see your kitchen because I'll need to prepare some food for after the funeral."

"I know," said Fell. "I could hire a catering firm."

"Might give them the idea you do have money. Do you have a microwave?"

"No, but I can buy one."

"We can buy lots of savouries and things from Marks and I can heat them up. Leave it to me. So what will you do? Travel?"

"I thought about that. But I don't want to see all that money drain away. Maybe I'll start some sort of business. Maybe a restaurant."

"A restaurant's a bit too much like what you've been doing for most of your life."

Fell smiled lazily at her, enjoying the unaccustomed effect of half a bottle of champagne and the heady relief of having been able to talk about himself at length with another human being. "What would you do, Maggie, if the money was yours?"

"I'm like you. Books are my solace, my friends. I would open a little bookshop with a coffee bar and a few tables at the back. I would have poetry readings, things like that. Oh, I'm being silly."

"We could do it!" said Fell, suddenly excited.

"We?" said Maggie faintly.

"Maybe you want to keep on at the hotel."

"God, no. Could we actually do it?"

"Why not?" Fell spread his arms. "There's so much we can do. Maggie, you've listened and listened to me. I know nothing about your life. Tell me."

"I'm trapped a bit like you were," said Maggie, "but not because my mother's possessive—far from it—but out of fear of living, fear of taking risks, lack of money. I've two older sisters—they're married. Mum has various men friends, who sometimes stay the night. She's got a sharp tongue. She runs me down a bit."

Perhaps it was the champagne or Maggie's worried and suddenly depressed face that made Fell say, "Move in with me."

She stared at him.

"Well, why not? It's a new century. We're friends."

"I'm beginning to feel as if I've been run over by a truck," said Maggie.

"We'll respect each other's space," said Fell. "I've promised my aunt Agnes all the furniture from the house. I want new stuff, light and airy."

"And everything clean," breathed Maggie.

"Oh, it's always been clean."

"My home's a tip. I keep my own room clean, but Mum has the rest of the place in a mess. I try clearing up after her, but lately I've given it up as a bad job."

"So why don't you just give up your job at the hotel?"

"Just like that?"

"Just like that. I need you, Maggie."

"Is this a real proposal?" asked Maggie with a light laugh.

Suddenly the old Fell was looking at her, his face wary and tight and set.

"I was only joking, Fell," said Maggie quickly. "We're friends, right? No funny business. Just friends."

Fell looked relieved. "Just friends."

"I'll go and powder my nose."

Maggie went through to the ladies' room and leaned against the handbasin. "The Maggies of this world," she told her reflection severely, "must take what they can get."

But a dry sob like that of a hurt child escaped her lips. She firmly reapplied her make-up and went back to join Fell.

It turned out that Maggie owned a small car, something Fell had not known before. She went home to fetch it, asking Fell to wait for her. It was too soon for him to meet her mother.

When Maggie returned with a suitcase of clothes they went out and bought a microwave and then loaded up the car with savouries from Marks.

As they unloaded the stuff in the kitchen, Fell said ruefully, "I'll need to buy a new fridge. There's hardly room in this little thing for all the stuff."

They had also bought bottles of various drinks and glasses. Maggie bustled about, examining everything. "How many relatives do you have?" she asked.

"Very few," said Fell. "There's Aunt Agnes; she's a widow. Then there's Cousin Tom and my other cousin, Barbara, and her husband, Fred. That's all."

"I hope they're hungry. We've bought rather a lot."

"We could eat some of it tonight and open a bottle of wine."

"Right. Which room shall I take?"

"I'll take my parents' room and you can have mine. What did your mother say?"

Maggie blushed. "She was out, so I left a note."

"She'll be round here any minute."

"I didn't tell her where I was going. I said I would phone her."

"Better get it over with," said Fell. "The phone's over there."

"Is that the famous desk?"

"Yes. Phone first and then we'll take a proper look through it."

Maggie phoned her mother. The conversation seemed to be very one-sided, with Maggie saying, "But . . . well, you see, it all happened suddenly. But . . ." At last she replaced the receiver. "She's furious. She says she needs my rent."

"Will she manage?"

"Of course she will. I'll need to get some sort of job, Fell. I can't live off you."

"Oh, I'll arrange money for you," said Fell expansively. "We'll be starting our business soon. I mean, just help yourself to what you need out of the cash box."

"Desk?"

"Yes, let's have a look."

Fell sorted out bank books and statements. "Nothing odd here," said Maggie. "Except for one thing."

"What?"

"Well, since you started work, your pay has been deposited each week. But there are no withdrawals. I mean they would have to draw money for bills, council tax, electricity, gas, things like that. There's not one withdrawal. And you said they gave you an allowance."

"That's odd. You would have thought the tax people would have been after them."

"Probably saw no reason to. Your tax was deducted from your earnings. What did they live on?"

"There must have been more money, much more than the money in the cash box."

"Is it exactly fifty thousand?"

Fell opened the cash box. "Just under. It's in bundles of twenties, see? I just counted the bundles." He flicked through them.

"Maybe they had rich relatives."

"I don't know of any. They scrimped and saved. We never even had holidays."

"There must be something in your past to explain it. Is there a photo album anywhere?"

"I don't remember seeing one."

"There aren't even any wedding or baby photos anywhere," said Maggie, looking around the dingy room.

"Let's look in my mother's room. I haven't had the heart to pack anything up."

They went up the stairs. The bedroom was as dark as the rest of the house. It was dominated by a large double bed. There was a dressing table by the window, with a hard chair in front of it. The fireplace had been blocked up. An Edwardian wardrobe took up most of one wall.

Fell opened the wardrobe. His mother had possessed few clothes. A wave of mothball smell made him wrinkle his nose. On the shelf above the hanging clothes were various hats. "We should get boxes after the funeral and pack all this up," said Maggie. "Take it all round to Oxfam."

"There's something behind the hats," said Fell, feeling with his fingers. He pulled out an old photo album.

He took it over to the bed. Maggie sat down beside him as

he opened it. There was a wedding photograph. To his surprise, his mother looked small and dainty and pretty. His father was stiff in new clothes and sported a large walrus moustache. "Why did they never show me this?" wondered Fell. "Here's another one of Dad at work. There's the signal box."

He had a sudden sharp memory of walking with his mother across the railway tracks to the signal box one hot summer's day. Willow herb grew along the verges by the railway lines and the air was redolent with the railway smell of soot and creosote.

There was a photo of his father standing on the platform with other railway workers. Then there was a photo of a couple having tea on the lawn outside a large mansion. They were an elderly, aristocratic-looking pair.

"Who are they? And where's that?" asked Maggie.

"I don't know," said Fell, bewildered.

There were various other photographs of trains and railway workers, and then nothing more.

"There isn't a photograph of you," exclaimed Maggie. "How very strange."

"I'll ask Aunt Agnes tomorrow if she's got any photos. Let's leave all this, Maggie. I've had enough for one day."

They spent the rest of the evening sharing a bottle of wine and watching television.

Then Fell looked out clean sheets and made up the bed for himself in his mother's room and changed the bed in his own room for Maggie.

"I hope you'll be all right," he said awkwardly.

"I'll be fine," said Maggie.

Fell lay awake for a long time. He tried to remember some affection in his childhood, some hugs and kisses, but could recall none. He prayed for the repose of his mother's soul and then asked forgiveness because he could not mourn her passing.

Maggie also lay awake for a long time, bewildered at the change in her circumstances. Had she been in love with Fell for a long time? He was the only person who had taken pains to be kind to her. Maggie had taken to reading adventure and spy stories so that they could have more to talk about in the hotel dining room. And yet she had never thought of having sex with him. When she was younger, she had experienced two brief flings, one in the back of a car with a businessman, the other with a wine salesman. Both episodes had left her feeling dirty and diminished. Now all she could think of was how much she really wanted Fell to love her and for him to make love to her. Perhaps they would grow together. But she knew in her bones that it would be very easy to frighten him off.

TWO

†

THE funeral of Mrs. Doris Dolphin took place on a beautiful morning in late May. The sun shone down on the churchyard with its old leaning tombstones, on the laburnum tree heavy with yellow blossoms by the church gate and on the dandelions that starred the thick tussocky grass.

The church of St. Peter's was very old, a Norman church built on Saxon foundations. The stained-glass windows had survived Cromwell's purges: splashes of jewelled colour lay across the pews and the stone-flagged aisle.

Despite the glory of the day, Aunt Agnes was buttoned tightly into a tweed coat. The coffin lay before the altar with one wreath of flowers supplied by Fell on the top.

Although the vicar had kept to Fell's choice of hymns, they were played by a steel band. How his mother would have hated it, thought Fell.

After the service, they drove in one large limousine—Barbara and her husband, Cousin Tom, Aunt Agnes, Fell and Maggie—behind the hearse to the town cemetery.

Maggie in a severe black suit looked the only one of them dressed for the occasion. Fell was wearing his new blazer and trousers with a black tie; Cousin Tom had on a blue suit and red tie, Barbara a yellow trouser suit, and her husband, Fred, the same sort of blue suit as Cousin Tom had on.

Fell tried to conjure up suitable feelings, but he felt numb and cold despite the increasing heat of the day. Must order a headstone, he thought.

There had been no conversation among them, but when they got back to the house and Maggie put on an apron and went off to the kitchen to heat the savouries, Fell poured drinks all round, regretting having lavished so much money on such a large selection because Barbara, Fred, Tom and Aunt Agnes all asked for sweet sherry.

"So that's your fiancée," began Aunt Agnes. "Not much of a looker, is she?"

"I find her very attractive," said Fell.

"Oh, well, I've never been able to make out what folks see in each other."

Fell set himself first to discovering if his relatives were in straitened circumstances. As Maggie handed around plates of savouries, he unearthed that Fred owned an electrical-goods shop in Cardiff, and Tom had a building business in Bath. Aunt Agnes said that she hoped Fell would manage. Her late husband, she said, had left her comfortably off. She didn't suppose Fell had been left much, she said, her little eyes bright with curiosity. Poor Doris had always complained they couldn't even afford a holiday.

Fell murmured that he would manage. He still insisted on sending the furniture to Aunt Agnes, but instead of saying this time that Maggie didn't like it, he said instead that it all reminded him of his dead parents.

Barbara and Fred looked bored and said they had better be getting back. "Oh, have another drink . . . just one," begged Fell. "I want to ask you all something. I can't find any family photographs. Have you got any of me when I was young, Aunt Agnes?"

"Can't say I have," said Aunt Agnes. "When are you getting married?"

"We're in no hurry," said Fell. "Wait here. I've something to show you."

He ran upstairs and got the photo album and returned with it. He opened it and took out the photo of the couple in front of the grand house. "Do you recognize them?"

"No," said Barbara. "What about you, Tom?"

"Never seen them before."

"Aunt Agnes?"

"Well, I'd better be going. Tom's offered me a lift to back home."

"But do you recognize them?"

"No. What do you want to bother about a lot of old photographs for, Fell?"

"Because I find it odd that there aren't any of me as a child."

"That was Doris for you. Never could abide getting her photo took. Now, Tom, if you're ready. . . ."

Maggie and Fell were alone. "That's that," said Fell, but he felt flat and disappointed. Ever a romantic, his busy imagination had begun to weave stories about that aristocratic couple in the photograph. Perhaps he had been adopted. Perhaps the elderly couple in the photograph were his real grandparents. Maybe their daughter had fallen pregnant to someone unsuitable. His father, he remembered, was always bragging about some "nob" or other he had chatted to on the platform. What if old Lord Thingummy had paid him to adopt the daughter's unwanted baby?

"Penny for them," said Maggie.

Fell gave a reluctant laugh and told her about his fantasy.

"I don't know," said Maggie slowly. "I often used to dream I was adopted. Unhappy children usually do."

"I suppose you're right." Fell looked downcast.

"I tell you what we could do," said Maggie quickly. "Once we've got this place fixed up, we could get a book on country houses and see if we can find one that looks like the one in the photograph."

Fell brightened. "We could do that. Then we'll see about setting up some business or other."

"The bookshop?"

"Or maybe a restaurant."

"Like I said, wouldn't that be a bit like what we've always done—waiting table?"

"We'll think about it. I mean, the glorious thing, Maggie, is we don't really need to work for a bit."

There was a ring at the door. "Now who can that be?" Fell rose and went to the door.

A hard-faced, middle-aged blonde stood on the doorstep. "I'm Maggie's mother," she said harshly.

"Come in." All at once, as he stood aside and she walked

past him, Fell realized he hadn't changed at all. Nothing had changed. He felt weak and cowed.

Mrs. Partlett sat down and crossed her legs. She was wearing a short tight skirt which rode up about her thighs. Her muscular legs ended in high-heeled sandals. A low-cut blouse plunged down to reveal the tops of two flabby breasts, pushed up by her brassiere. Her mouth was painted scarlet, and her discontented face was floury with white powder dusted over some sort of heavy foundation cream with which she had attempted to grout the wrinkles in her face.

She lit a cigarette and blew smoke in Maggie's direction. Another stereotype, thought Fell. The world is full of stereotypes. She's like a stage tart.

"So what are you up to, girl?" asked Mrs. Partlett.

"I've moved in with Fell. We're going to get married."

"Oh, yeah? Where's the ring?"

"We're going to get one . . . soon."

Fell noticed that Maggie wasn't wearing the emerald ring.

"I met that wop from the hotel bar," said Mrs. Partlett. "He told me you'd both jacked in your jobs. What are you going to live on?"

"I've got a little money," said Fell.

"Won't last long. You'll need to provide for her."

"It's got nothing to do with you," said Maggie, turning blotchy red with anger. "You've never bothered about my welfare before."

"Don't get snippy with me. No one going to offer me a drink?"

"No," said Maggie, getting to her feet. "We're just going out."

Mrs. Partlett rose to her feet. She'll wriggle her hips and

smooth down her skirt, thought Fell. Mrs. Partlett did just that.

She turned on Fell. "I'll be keeping my eye on you, and do you know why? I think you're a pervert."

"How dare you!" shouted Maggie.

Her mother looked at her with scorn. "What man's ever been interested in you before? Oh, don't give me your lies about Tom, Dick or Harry who died or went abroad. I knew they were lies. I know just about everyone in this town."

"You should," said Maggie evenly. "You've slept with most of them."

Mrs. Partlett shrugged her shoulders and walked to the door. "You never really grew up, Maggie. I'll be watching you."

She went out and slammed the door behind her.

Maggie collapsed into a chair and began to cry.

Fell circled helplessly around her, saying, "Don't cry. She's gone." He knelt down in front of her and took her hands in his. "I know, let's get out of here. Take me for a drive."

"Where?"

"Anywhere, and where's your ring?"

Maggie fished in her pocket and drew out the ring and put it on. "I took it off as soon as I knew it was her. If she saw it, she would smell money and we'd never be rid of her."

When they were driving along the country lanes, Fell said, "Was she always like that?"

"I suppose so," said Maggie wearily. "My sisters are like her. I was the bookish one. I always felt like a stranger in my own home."

"Never mind. Listen to me, Maggie. The old part of our lives is over. We've never really had any fun."

"Maybe it's too late for us."

"Don't say that," exclaimed Fell, suddenly furious with her because he feared what she said might be true.

But during the following weeks, thoughts of adoption and worries about where the money in the cash box might have come from were temporarily forgotten as Fell and Maggie, once they had cleared the house of all the old furniture, set to work. Fell decided his idea of turning the living room into a kitchen was too ambitious. He quickly ordered a modern three-piece suite for the living room, then he and Maggie concentrated on refurbishing the old kitchen. All the old units were taken out—the fridge, the ancient washing machine, and the inadequate cooker. They ripped off the old wallpaper and painted the walls sparkling white. They ordered the kitchen counter complete with stainless-steel sinks and cupboard from a D.I.Y. store. Fell assured Maggie that all they had to do was study the instructions and they could do it all themselves, although by the time they had bought a whole range of expensive electrical tools, Maggie privately thought it would have been cheaper to pay the shop extra to fit it for them. They ripped up the old green linoleum and found a stone-flagged floor underneath.

"You'll need to get some new clothes," said Fell, watching Maggie scrubbing the flags.

"Why?" demanded Maggie defensively.

Fell laughed. "It's all this exercise. You've lost a lot of weight."

It was not only the exercise. Maggie had always eaten comfort food—chocolate puddings, piles of pasta, anything to fill the empty spiritual hole inside. But Fell had become a gourmet, wanting to get as far away from his mother's "good plain cooking" as possible. The weather was becoming increasingly hot and they had been eating a lot of salads.

"You could take a break, and we could go and get you something," suggested Fell.

"Do you want to come with me?"

"Why not? I've never had the experience of watching a woman choose clothes. Let's go to Cheltenham. They've got some really smart shops in the Parade."

To Maggie, it was a delight to try on pretty dresses and find that they fitted. Before, she had always chosen skirts with elasticated waists and loose blouses or sweaters to hide her lumpy shape.

Fell bought a charcoal grey suit, shirts and new underwear until, after several trips back to the car park, Maggie's little car was laden.

"Now, let's get your hair done," said Fell.

"I don't think much can be done with it."

"It's shiny now. It didn't use to be," said Fell. "Let's try."

Maggie had her dreams and fantasies as well. When she emerged from the hairdresser with her hair cut in a becoming wispy feathery cut which framed her heart-shaped face, she felt it was only a matter of time now before she and Fell became lovers. He was so delighted with her appearance.

They decided to dress up in their new clothes that evening and go out to the French restaurant.

Maggie put on a fine cotton dress, white with a pattern of roses which clung to her now shapely hips and was long enough to hide her legs. She pictured the scene in the restaurant. There would be candlelight in the evening and Fell would lean across the table and look into her eyes and take her hand, and then . . . and then . . .

She thought Fell looked distinguished and handsome in his new suit and striped shirt. Well content with each other, they walked through the balmy summer evening to the restaurant. Swallows swooped around the walls of the old castle.

"Dandelion summer," said Fell. "It's a dandelion summer."

Together they went into the restaurant. Bolder now, Maggie ordered her own food. The next step in her appearance was contact lenses.

Fell smiled into her eyes.

"What are you thinking?" asked Maggie huskily.

Fell laughed. "I was thinking that I can't wait to start on the living room tomorrow. We've been using that packing case as a table for long enough."

It's too soon, Maggie chided herself, as the bubble of her dream burst. I mustn't rush things.

"That woman over there, the one who keeps smiling over at me," said Fell. "I know her from somewhere."

Maggie followed his gaze. "That's Mrs. Harley. Used to dine at the hotel with her husband. I heard he died last year."

"What did her husband do?"

"He was manager of your bank."

Mrs. Harley rose and walked over to their table. She was the sort of woman, Fell thought, that he often dreamed about. She was wearing a short black chiffon dress which clung to her excellent figure and showed off her long, long legs. Fell saw a cloud of dark hair, a full pouting mouth and large dark eyes fringed with long lashes.

"I know you, don't I?" she said to Fell.

All at once, Fell wished he were on his own. He knew he

would never have told her he had been a waiter at the Palace.

But there was Maggie, and Maggie was saying, "We both waited table at the Palace."

"Of course!" She smiled. "You look so . . . debonair . . . I didn't recognize you."

"I'm Fellworth Dolphin, Fell, and this is Maggie Partlett. I was sorry to hear about your husband's death," said Fell.

"Yes, too sad. I'm in business now. Let me give you my card. I run a health shop in the High Street." She handed Fell a card. "Drop in and see me and we can have a chat."

She drifted off on a cloud of Chanel.

Maggie's dreams lay in ruins. Fell was looking excited, happy, elated, and his eyes kept drifting over to Mrs. Harley's table.

"I hope our Mrs. Harley is not a gold-digger," said Maggie with a lightness she did not feel.

"Why should she be that?"

"This is a small town and gossip travels fast. It's a good thing your relatives don't live here. A lot of people probably know now that you've come into money."

Fell frowned. "She seems very prosperous."

Maggie dropped the subject and tried to chat about house improvements and ignore the heavy, indigestible misery that had settled somewhere in her gut.

To her relief, Mrs. Harley left. Immediately Fell decided they should get home. Usually he liked to linger over his coffee.

And once home, he didn't want to sit up. He was tired, he said. And Maggie knew he wanted to be alone with dreams of Mrs. Harley.

In his room, Fell took out that precious card. Her full name was Melissa Harley. He had fallen in love before with such as Melissa, but his circumstances had kept his love to fantasies and dreams. He dreamt like a very young teenager, for his repressive life had frozen his emotional development like an insect in amber.

But he was blessed with a certain amount of stoic common sense, and in the clear light of another morning, all he looked forward to was more home improvements with Maggie.

It was only after another busy morning of shopping and planning, when Maggie suddenly said she had left her television set, but might as well go and get it and then they would have one each, that he felt the compulsion to go out and stroll along the High Street in the direction of the health shop.

The shop was called Whole Body and as he hesitated outside the window, Melissa Harley came out. "Why, if it isn't Fellworth," she said.

"Fell," he corrected quickly. "I don't like my name much." He blinked a little in the sunlight. Melissa seemed smaller and plumper than he remembered, but Fell was a romantic and he wanted to see a glamorous woman again, and so his imagination quickly told him that he did.

"Why did your parents choose a name like that?"

"They never told me. I suffered a lot because of it at school."

"Poor you. Got time for a coffee?"

Of course he had. All the time in the world.

They strolled into a tea shop of the olde English variety, beams and horse brasses, and cakes that most of the world had forgotten about—Eiffel towers, congress cake, fly cemeteries, empire biscuits.

She fixed those dark eyes on his and said in her husky voice, "Tell me about yourself."

"There's not much to tell," said Fell. "I've had a rather dreary life."

"You're not still waiting table?"

"No, my parents have left me a bit of money, so I've packed it in."

"So what do you plan to do?"

"I thought of starting up some sort of business, a restaurant or bookshop."

She smiled at him, a languorous smile. "Or you could invest in an existing business—like mine."

He stared at her. "Would you like to work with me, Fell? I run a prosperous little concern."

"That would be wonderful. But I'd need to ask Maggie."

"Ah, yes, your little friend. Well, let me know." She was suddenly brisk. Fell longed to tell her that his engagement to Maggie was a sham, but an irritating loyalty to Maggie kept him quiet.

She talked about the shop, about how she had dreamt up the idea after her husband died. Fell looked through the distorting prism of his imagination at what he saw as the beauty of her face and listened to the sound of her voice, mesmerized.

When they parted, he braced himself to tell Maggie. Maggie would be disappointed because she was really keen on a bookshop, but it was *his* money and Maggie would just need to get used to the idea.

Maggie was home when he arrived. To his relief, she did not protest, simply listened to him quietly with her hands folded. "It's your inheritance," said Maggie when he had finished. "You haven't had much fun in your life. You have to do exactly what you want."

Fell hugged her in a sudden rush of gratitude. "I know you really wanted a bookshop, Maggie, but this is a going business. But I'm not going to do anything at the moment. I'll wait a bit."

"Sure," said Maggie, detaching herself gently. "I'm just going up to my room. I haven't quite decided which paint to get."

Maggie went upstairs and closed the bedroom door behind her. She sat down on the bed. She knew, she was sure, that Mrs. Melissa Harley was after Fell's money. But there was no way to prove it. She had a sudden desire to watch Melissa covertly. She went downstairs and told Fell that she was going to call on her mother. Fell was busy unwrapping china and only nodded.

Maggie went out into the golden glory of the summer's evening. She felt small and grubby and toadlike. She looked up at the clock on the town hall. The health shop would be closing soon, Melissa would be locking up, and Maggie could get a clear, calm look at the woman she considered her rival. She took up a position in a doorway opposite the health shop and waited. Five-thirty. A shop girl came out and walked off down the street. Maggie shifted restlessly.

" 'Allo, Maggie."

She found the grinning face of the Italian barman, Gino, from the Palace two inches from her own.

"Waiting for a pick-up?"

"I'm waiting for a friend," muttered Maggie. "Go away."

Gino was handsome and knew it. He was wearing his off-duty clothes of leather jacket and jeans with gold chains nestling in his chest hair. He smelt overpoweringly of Brut.

"So you've moved in with the drip," said Gino.

"Go *away!*" hissed Maggie.

Gino patted her on the bottom and walked off, whistling.

Maggie saw Melissa Harley emerge. She looked tired. Her hair was screwed up on a knot on top of her head. She was wearing a trouser suit and flat shoes. Her jacket was open, revealing a slightly bulging stomach.

She must have been wearing a body stocking last night, thought Melissa. And she's not really beautiful at all. It was only my jealousy that made her appear beautiful.

Feeling comforted, she headed homeward.

But Maggie did not realize that Fell only saw the Melissa he wanted to see, and that was the glamorous woman of his dreams. She realized later that she should have said nothing. But as soon as she was in the door, she burst out with, "I saw Melissa Harley in the High Street."

Fell's face brightened. "Did you talk to her?"

"No, I just saw her, and Fell, she's quite old and not that good-looking. She must have been wearing some sort of foundation garment when we saw her in the restaurant, because she's got a bulgy figure and I think she must be near fifty."

Fell's face darkened. "You didn't go to your mother. You went to spy."

And instead of denying it hotly, Maggie said miserably, "I only went to get another look at her. I'm worried about you, Fell. I think she's after your money."

Fell rose to his feet. His face was closed and set and bleak. "I'm going out for a walk," he said.

"I—I'm s-sorry," babbled Maggie, "but I couldn't bear to see you tricked."

"Yes, quite," said Fell and walked out of the door.

He walked and walked that evening along by the river. He walked until his legs were as weary as his soul. He felt a dull hatred for Maggie. How dare Maggie interfere in his dreams? Well, he was not going to be chained to Maggie the way he had been chained to his parents. He was not swapping one prison for another. He would tell her in the morning she had to go. It was his house and his life.

Maggie lay awake, waiting for him to return. If only she had never criticized Melissa. If only she had denied spying on her. But Fell was so naïve. She heard Fell come in. Somehow Maggie felt his feelings seeping through the walls of her room. The fun was over. Fell would never forgive her. She would have to leave. Back to Mother, back to waitressing, back to empty days and lonely nights.

She remembered that enchanted meal in the restaurant, where she had put on the ring, where she had been happier than she had ever been in her life before, and she turned her face into the pillow and wept.

Maggie cried so hard that it was some time before she realized someone was knocking at the downstairs door.

She sat up and scrubbed her eyes dry with a corner of the sheet. She heard Fell open his bedroom door and go down the stairs. Maggie climbed out of bed and put on her dressing gown. She crept quietly downstairs and stood, listening.

Fell opened the door. A huge figure stood silhouetted against the street light outside.

"You Fellworth Dolphin, Charlie's boy?" asked a gruff voice.

"Yes; what do you want?"

"I'm Tarry Joe's boy. Let me in."

"Why should I?" Fell remembered that Tarry Joe had been a railway worker at the station in his father's day.

"Want me to talk about the robbery on the step?"

Maggie moved swiftly to the desk and took out the cash box as she heard Fell exclaiming, "What robbery? I don't know anything about a robbery."

Maggie let herself out of the back door into the garden. The new gardening equipment was lying about, along with plants from a gardening centre for the newly weeded garden.

She seized a spade and dug a hole in the soft earth and dropped the cash box into it, shovelled earth over it, and patted it flat. Then she crept back into the kitchen. She could now hear voices in the living room. "Anyone want a cup of tea?" she called.

There was a silence and then the man said sharply, "Who's that?"

Maggie walked into the living room and said brightly, "I heard someone arrive, Fell, and I thought you might like a cup of tea."

Her eyes quickly took in the visitor. Massive and brawny in a denim shirt with cut-off sleeves exposing tattooed arms, a bullet-like head with small babyish features crammed in the middle of a large face.

"Who's this?"

"My fiancée, Maggie," said Fell in a dazed voice. "Maggie, this man . . ." He looked helplessly at Tarry Joe's son.

"Andy. Andy Briggs."

"Andy," said Fell, "says my father was part of a plan to rob a train. Andy here is looking for a place to stay. He also wants money."

"Why should we give him any?" asked Maggie.

"Because," said Fell in a thin voice, "he says he has proof of my father's involvement in the robbery and if we don't pay him, he'll go to the police."

Maggie came in and sat down. "What robbery?" she asked. "When did it happen?"

"It was over twenty years ago," Andy said. "Never heard of the Post Office train robbery?"

"I remember that," said Fell. "There was a trainload of used notes being taken from the North back down to the central post office in London. The train was attacked by masked men at Buss Station." His voice sharpened. "The guard was bludgeoned to death. They never caught anyone."

"That's right. My father went to Spain with his cut, took me with him, and the silly sod drank himself to death. Your father got his cut for tipping us off about the train and looking the other way."

"Fell's father's dead," said Maggie.

"Heard that," said Andy laconically. His small eyes focused on Fell. "Don't want the world to know your dad was a criminal."

"I don't mind," said Fell. "Go to the police."

"Then let me put it another way, sonny," said Andy. He had a duffel bag at his feet. He bent down and opened it. He pulled out an old service revolver. "You get me the money. I've been dossing in this town and know you've been left a mint. So we go to the bank in the morning and you pay up or I'll blow your brains out." Andy swung round on Maggie. "And you go and get me tea and some sandwiches. One false move and I'll kill your boyfriend."

Maggie rose and went into the kitchen.

Fell stared numbly at Andy. Fell had been brought up on threats that God would punish him if he was bad, a God of wrath, a God with long flowing locks and a long beard. He felt he was being punished for having kept that money in the cash box. He felt weak with fear. He could feel his knees trembling under his dressing gown. He was sure he was about to wet himself. He could have cried with weakness and shame and fright.

In some of his many fantasies, he had been threatened by a gunman, but had disarmed him with one karate chop. He prayed that Maggie had somehow run out of the kitchen door for help.

But the kitchen door opened and he heard Maggie say brightly, "Tea's ready."

Andy was sitting with his back to the table where Maggie placed the tray.

"Don't move," he said to Fell with a grin and Fell knew that Andy was well aware that he, Fell, was too frightened to move a muscle.

In the same moment, as in a dream, Fell saw Maggie lift a marble rolling pin off the tea tray. Just as Andy was about to rise to his feet, Maggie brought the rolling pin down on his bullet head with all the force given to her by fear.

Andy gave a choked sound and tumbled forward onto the carpet. Fell leaped out of his chair and grabbed the gun from Andy's limp hand. Blood was oozing from the back of Andy's head onto the carpet.

Fell sat down on the sofa and levelled the gun at the recumbent Andy. Maggie stood shaking, her hands to her mouth. Then she crept round and sat down next to Fell.

"We can't let him bleed to death," she whispered.

"Give it a minute," Fell whispered back. "He may be faking."

"What, with all that blood?"

"Okay, have a look at him."

Maggie shuddered. "I can't. Oh, I can't. You have a look at him."

Fell handed her the gun, but it dropped from Maggie's nervous fingers to the carpet.

Fell picked up the gun and put it in a drawer. Then he got down on his knees and shuffled over to the body. He felt Andy's wrist. No pulse.

"I think he's dead, Maggie."

"He can't be. Oh, what are we to do?"

"I don't know," said Fell helplessly. "Maybe we should call for an ambulance."

"Then I'd be a murderess and the court would take all your money."

"If the money comes from a robbery, then they'll need to have it."

"But what if he was bluffing? What if your father had nothing to do with it at all?"

"Let's look in that bag of his," said Fell.

They tipped out the contents of the bag. It contained dirty laundry, a long knife, a passport, and a driving licence.

Fell sat back on his heels.

"I think he would have taken my money and killed us both. What if . . . what if we just got rid of the body and then tried to find out ourselves if Dad really had anything to do with that robbery?"

"Should we put the body in the boot of my car and dump it in the river?"

"No," said Fell. "Let's bury him in the garden. Thank God he arrived in the middle of the night. Let's hope no one saw him. Anyway, we'll just need to hope he's not reported missing. I need to pee."

“Me too,” said Maggie. “You first.”

After they had both finished with the bathroom, they went outside to the garden. For once Fell blessed his parents’ desire to “keep ourselves to ourselves.” A high hedge on both sides of the garden blocked off any view from the neighbouring houses. A tall lilac tree to the left shut most of the view from the windows next door on that side and a holly tree on the right shielded the view from there.

“I buried the cash box,” said Maggie. “It’s over there. Where will we put him?”

“Close to the house. No danger of being seen that way.”

They both took up new spades and began to dig. “My arms ache,” complained Maggie.

“It’s got to be deep,” said Fell. “We don’t want stray cats or dogs digging it up.”

The sky began to lighten and the first birds twittered from the trees.

“That’s good enough,” said Fell at last.

They leaned on their shovels and looked at each other across the open grave, their faces white and strained in the growing light.

“Better get him,” said Fell wearily. “We’ll take the wheelbarrow. You hold open the kitchen door for me, Maggie.”

Maggie held open the door. Fell pushed the wheelbarrow inside the kitchen. With Maggie behind him, he opened the living-room door.

He let out a gasp.

The only sign of Andy was a dried pool of blood on the carpet. The street door was standing open. The duffel bag was gone.

“He can’t have been dead!” said Fell.

“Thank God,” said Maggie, and began to cry.

THREE

†

THEY slept a little. Maggie awoke, hearing Fell downstairs. She rose and dressed, hurriedly and without care.

Fell was sitting over a cup of coffee, staring into space.

"I don't know what to do, Maggie," he said bleakly.

Despite the fact that she was still terrified by the events of the night, Maggie knew in that moment that she had gained a reprieve. Fell would not throw her out, not immediately anyway.

"Do you think he'll come back?" asked Maggie.

"Possibly. It's a nightmare. Why did I never remember the robbery when I saw the money in the cash box? It was right after that Dad had his first heart attack. I was set to go to university, but I had to stay at the Palace instead. I'd been working at the hotel in my gap year and so I just stayed on."

"Let's go out somewhere in my car for breakfast," said Maggie briskly, "and then we'll go to the library and read up on everything we can about the robbery."

"What should I do with that gun?"

"I'll put it up in my room in the suitcase under the bed. Let's go, Fell. If we sit here, I'll get too frightened to move at all."

"Right." Fell went to the drawer, took out the gun and handed it to Maggie, who took it gingerly. She went back to her room and tucked it at the bottom of an old suitcase.

They went out to Maggie's car, which was parked outside. The sun shone down on another perfect day.

"Mr. Dolphin!" quavered an old voice from the front garden on their right.

"Mrs. Moule," said Fell. He raised his voice. "Good morning."

Mrs. Moule appeared at her gate, leaning on a Zimmer frame. "You young people," she chided. "I don't know where you get the energy. Digging the garden in the middle of the night."

"That's us," said Fell with a manufactured breeziness. "Working all hours to make the place nice."

Mrs. Moule cackled with laughter. "Well, if you've any energy left over, my garden could do with weeding."

Fell waved. He and Maggie got into the car. Maggie drove off and then stopped farther down the road. "Wait a bit," she said. "My knees are shaking. Just think, Fell. What if we *had* been burying a body? How could she have seen us?"

"Probably heard us or saw us through the branches of that tree outside the upstairs window. It was getting light, remember?"

"I wonder whether we should go to the police," said Maggie.

"It's a bit late for that, Maggie. They'd wonder why we didn't call them immediately. And what if they froze the money in the bank? We'd lose our first bit of freedom."

Maggie privately though they had lost it already, but he had said *our* freedom, and that was enough for her.

She let in the clutch. "Where are we going?" asked Fell.

"I thought we'd go out to one of those motorway restaurants and eat junk food, comfort food, for once."

"You're a good sort, Maggie."

Maggie felt the sunlight outside flooding her insides with yellow light. But she felt she had to say something about Melissa Harley.

"About Melissa," said Maggie. "I feel now I behaved disgracefully. I wasn't trying to isolate you from people, Fell." *Lie,* screamed the voice of her conscience. "But I just didn't want to see you tricked."

Fell sighed. "I suppose you think a woman who looks like that would never be interested in me."

"Not at all," said Maggie quickly.

"I was hurt," said Fell. "Badly hurt by your snooping. But the events of last night have made me pretty much forget about it."

"Let's not talk any more about it at the moment," said Maggie, negotiating a roundabout and turning down onto the motorway.

"I've had about two driving lessons," said Fell. "But I can't imagine myself ever driving on a motorway. Look at them! The inside lane does seventy miles an hour. But the middle lane does eighty and the outside lane ninety or more."

"You get used to it," said Maggie. "When I first started driving, I would keep to the inside lane and just chug along behind the trucks."

After several miles, she turned off at a motorway restaurant.

Soon they were seated over enormous breakfasts of toast, eggs, bacon, mushrooms, beans and sausages.

"So if we can stay awake after this lot," said Maggie, "we'll go back to town and start at the library. Are any of your father's old workmates alive?"

"I'll need to ask around. Dad was pretty old when he died. I hate this. I don't know if I can live in my house again. I'll always be waiting for a knock at the door, dreading that Andy will come back."

"Let's not think about that now. But perhaps we should get some sort of security, a burglar-alarm system, something like that, and a peephole on the front door so we can see who is calling. We can look up the business pages in the directory for a security firm."

Maggie regretted the idea of a greasy breakfast although she finished every bit of it. She felt tired and heavy.

She drove them back into Buss and they parked outside the public library. "When was the robbery?" asked Maggie.

"It was sometime in the seventies. Wait a bit. They talked of nothing else in the town. Let's start with the local newspaper for 1978."

An hour later, after ploughing through pages and pages of a bound volume of the *Buss Courier,* they could find no mention of any railway robbery. "We could ask one of the old people in the town," said Maggie. "They'd remember."

"I don't want to draw attention to us."

"I'll ask the librarian. She won't be interested. So many people ask her for things, she won't remember us in particular."

"I don't know . . . ," began Fell doubtfully, but Maggie was already on her feet and moving to the desk. The librarian was a young girl in her twenties. She had real blonde hair and bright blue eyes. Maggie was glad it was she who had gone to ask and not Fell. Maggie's world was becoming peopled, she felt, with women who might lure Fell away.

"I'm looking for something on a train robbery which took place here," said Maggie.

"Oh, the Buss train robbery," said the girl with a smile. Those blue eyes were intelligent. No one that pretty ought to be intelligent as well.

"There was a book written about that by a local man," said the librarian, switching on the computer on her desk. "I'm sure it's out of print, but we might still have a copy because it's of local interest."

She flicked expertly at the machine. "Ah, here it is. *The Buss Train Robbery,* by Geoffrey Hobson. You'll find it actually in the section of local books. The number is P142."

Maggie went back to Fell, her face glowing with triumph. "Someone wrote a book on it," she told Fell. "Wait there and I'll get it."

She searched the shelves, and to her delight, located the book and brought it back to Fell.

"Can we borrow it?" she asked. "Do you have a library card?"

"Yes," said Fell, thinking what a refuge this library had been in his dark, lonely days: a world full of books of romance and adventure. The very smell of the books meant comfort. The dome in the ceiling of green glass shed an underwater light down into the library where submarine humans like himself wandered along the shelves seeking escape.

They decided to take the book down to the river bank and study it. The robbery had actually taken place in 1977. "I'm getting old," said Fell ruefully. "I should have remembered it was seventy-seven."

Holding the book between them and sitting on the grass by the river, they read steadily.

At last Fell said, “To summarize, the robbery took place at ten o’clock in the morning. The bit where my father comes in seems to be that the train was not due to stop at Buss but the signal was against it and so the train stopped. As soon as it stopped, five masked men attacked the train. There were only six Post Office employees, a train driver and a guard on board. The Post Office employees were threatened at gunpoint and tied up. The guard tried to escape and was beaten to death. It was estimated the robbers got away with five million. Dad was pulled in for questioning. He said he received a phone call telling him to stop the train. The call was traced to a phone box. Dad had an excellent record. Joe Briggs, Tarry Joe, was suspected because it turned out he had a criminal record, but he fled to Spain, and there was no extradition agreement between Britain and Spain then. The others were pulled in for questioning, and the ones I remember meeting when I went to see my father in the signal box were Fred Flint and Johnny Tremp, maintenance workers.”

“So where do we go from here? Didn’t your parents discuss it?” asked Maggie.

“Not a word. In fact, I don’t remember them actually talking much about anything. We’ll start with the phone book and see if Fred Flint and Johnny Tremp are still alive.”

“You would think the police would have caught at least one of them.”

“It says in the book that the police said it was planned like a military operation. They were looking for some sort of criminal with an army background.”

“It’s going to be awfully hard to find out anything after all this time,” said Maggie sadly.

“What amazes me is why Andy Briggs was not picked up

at the airport, or Dover or however he came back into the country."

"They'd be looking for Joe Briggs. Briggs is a common name. They wouldn't be looking for the son."

"You're right. Let's go home and look at the phone book."

Maggie hesitated. "I think we should take that book back to the library."

"Why? I would like to go through it again."

"It's like this. If Andy comes back and we're forced to call the police, they're going to put two and two together and maybe search the house. If they find this book, it'll start them thinking."

"You're right. Next time we want to check it, we'll read it in the library."

As they walked back across the grass, Maggie said, "You could always say you were writing a book about Buss and want to do a chapter on the train robbery. That would give us an excuse to go around asking questions. We could even try to find that local inspector who was on the case, the one from Buss; what was his name?"

"Inspector Rudfern. I could do that, Maggie."

They returned the book and headed home.

"Maybe I'd better buy a typewriter. Make it look as if I'm really writing," said Fell.

"No one bothers with typewriters these days. Get a computer with a word processor program."

"Wouldn't it take me forever to learn how to use it?"

"I think some people just follow the instructions."

Maggie parked outside the house. They both looked out at it uneasily as if expecting to see the burly figure of Andy waiting for them.

But when they walked in, there was only the smell of new paint to greet them.

"You know," said Fell, sitting down with a sigh, "I feel like a criminal. Everything points to Dad taking money from the robbers. Spending money is no longer going to be any fun. Every penny I spend now is going to feel as if I'm spending money that doesn't belong to me."

"Your wages your father banked over the years are yours."

"Yes, but the reason he was able to bank all of that money was maybe because of a robbery."

"Never mind. We'll find out what we can. Would you like me to get a job? That way you wouldn't have to spend so much."

"You're a kind girl, Maggie," said Fell, giving her a quick hug. "We're in this together, so we may as well spend together."

Maggie smiled shyly up at him. She no longer cared what mystery or mayhem they were involved in, just so long as they were together. The awful spectre that he might turn her out had gone.

The phone rang, a shrill and peremptory tone.

Fell jumped nervously. "Will I answer it?" asked Maggie.

"Please. My nerves are shot."

Maggie picked up the receiver. It was Melissa Harley.

"For you," she said bleakly and held out the receiver in answer to Melissa's request to speak to Fell. She watched Fell's face light up when he realized who it was. Then she heard him say, "I'd love to, but something's come up. Could we possibly make it for next week? . . . Great. I'll see you on Wednesday at eight."

He turned to Maggie, his face radiant. "She's invited me to her house for dinner. I'm to pick her up at the shop."

"I heard you put it off until next week," said Maggie. "Why?"

Fell ran his fingers through his hair. "I just want to be on top form when I see her. I'm still rattled after last night."

"Would you like a cup of coffee before we start on the phone book?" asked Maggie.

"Thank you," said Fell, his face bright with happiness.

Damn the conniving bitch, thought Maggie. She returned with two mugs of coffee and joined Fell on the sofa. "Who should we start with?" asked Fell.

"I think the inspector would be our best bet."

Fell opened the local phone book. "Let's see, Rudfern. What's his first name?"

"Oh, I can't remember."

"There's one here. Only one. J. J. Rudfern, 12, Glebe Close."

"Let's try him now," said Maggie eagerly, anxious for any action which would take Fell's mind off Melissa Harley.

"We'll have our coffee and then go," he said. "What were those other two names?"

"Fred Flint and Johnny Tremp."

"Right." He scanned the phone book again. "There's a J. Tremp but—let me see—no Fred Flint, or F. Flint. There's several Flints."

"We'll try them all later." Maggie rose. "I'll just wash my face. I'm still tired."

"After we see this inspector—if he's still alive—we can have a sleep."

How wonderful it would be, thought Maggie, if having a sleep meant they could tumble into bed together. She went up to the bathroom, which had not yet been renovated. The handbasin had a crack across it, and the old-fashioned bath was permanently stained with lime scale from a dripping tap.

The work on the house should go ahead. The new furniture in the living room looked too bright against the dingy walls. Keep Fell occupied, that was the plan. A fully occupied Fell would be less easy prey for rapacious women.

Maggie removed her heavy glasses and washed her face and then carefully applied fresh make-up. If only she could get contact lenses, but now, all this threat that the late Mr. Dolphin had actually been involved in crime made her too shy to ask Fell for the money.

Glebe Close was a cul-de-sac at the prosperous end of the town. It consisted of a few large villas with spacious gardens.

"I don't think we're going to have that dandelion summer of yours after all," said Maggie. "It's clouding over and getting quite chilly."

"Just a country story," said Fell. "I suppose they say it every year and the one year they get it right is the year everyone remembers."

They climbed out of the car. Fell pushed open one of the tall double iron gates and he and Maggie walked up a well-kept drive between laurel bushes, flowering black currant and rhododendrons.

After they had rung a brass bell set into the stone at the side of the door, a fashionably dressed middle-aged woman opened the door. She was wearing a tailored trouser suit in biscuit-coloured linen, high-heeled sandals, and a quantity of gold chains around her neck. Her eyes in her well-preserved face were hard and assessing. "Yes?"

"I am Fell Dolphin," said Fell, who never used his first name in full if he could help it, "and this is Miss Maggie Partlett."

"And?" The woman stood before them, one hip jutting out, one thin beringed hand splayed against it.

"I am writing a book on the Buss train robbery which took place in nineteen seventy-seven. I believe Inspector Rudfern was on that case. I just wanted to ask him about it."

She hesitated. Then she said, "I'll see if Father is up to talking." She turned back indoors and left them standing on the step. A rising wind rustled through the bushes behind them. The hum of traffic on the main road came faintly to their ears.

Then they heard the clack of returning high heels. "Come in," she said, "but don't stay too long."

They followed her into the gloomy hush of the large house. There seemed to be venetian blinds on all the windows, cutting out much of the light.

"Father's in the study," she said, pushing open the door.

A old man was sitting in an armchair by the window, a tartan travelling rug over his knees. He had a shock of grey hair, and a grey lined and wrinkled face from which faded blue eyes surveyed them curiously.

"Sit down," he said in a surprisingly strong voice. "Dolphin, my daughter said. That name rings a bell."

"Charles Dolphin, my father, was a signalman at the time of the robbery."

"Ah, so he was. Pulled in for questioning. Bring over two chairs and sit in front of me where I can see you."

With an effort Fell lifted over two carved high-backed chairs of the mock Tudor kind.

When he and Maggie were seated, Fell asked, "Why was he taken in for questioning?"

"Because that train with the Post Office money was not supposed to stop at Buss," said Mr. Rudfern. "He was the one who stopped it. Besides, it was his day off, but he volunteered to work it. The other signalman, Terry Weal, said he was feeling poorly and Dolphin had offered to do his shift."

"And what explanation did my father give for stopping the train?"

"He said he had received a phone call half an hour before the train was due to pass through Buss Station, which he had no reason to disbelieve, telling him the train must be stopped because a cracked wheel was suspected. We traced the call to the signal box. There was only the one and it came from a phone box outside Buss. Dolphin stuck to his story that he had been tricked. Then he was asked, as he had a phone in the signal box, why he didn't immediately call the police when the robbery started. He said that one of the men had a rifle pointed up at the signal box. He couldn't phone until they had gone."

"Why couldn't the man in the ticket office call?" asked Fell.

"There were no trains expected until later in the day, so the ticket office was closed. We decided to keep an eye on all the suspects, see if they started spending more money than they should have had. Dolphin didn't seem to have anything other than his wages, and then yours. Yes, we kept an eye on people for as long as that. The only one who splurged out was Briggs. We were moving in to pick him up when he disappeared to Spain. No extradition agreement, and by the time there was, the old sod was dead."

"No idea who did it?"

"None. But someone with a clever brain masterminded it."

"Is there any way my father could have known what was on the train?"

"On the face of it—no. But back up in Glasgow where they loaded up the train, some of the workers must have known what was on it, and the Post Office workers on the train certainly knew. Easy to leak the news."

"I read a book about it by a local author," said Fell. "He says it was as if some sort of ghost squad had performed the robbery and just melted away. No one saw any cars racing away from the station."

"No one much around there except at train times," said Rudfern. "Not like in the cities, you know. In country places, the station's often well outside the town, like in Buss. I read that book. Silly piece of reporting. Great gaps in it. We hauled in all known criminals from miles around. We have our snouts—informers—so we waited, sure that some whisper would come out of the underworld. Nothing. You know what I think?"

Maggie and Fell leaned forward. Mr. Rudfern's daughter came in. "Are you finished yet?" she demanded. "Father needs his rest."

"Go away," said Mr. Rudfern. "Now!"

She went out, slamming the door behind her. "It's terrible to be old and be at the mercy of your children," said the ex-inspector, half to himself. "Where was I?"

"You were about to tell us what you thought," said Maggie eagerly.

"Yes. Well, no one would listen to me. But it's this. I think it was masterminded by someone with military training and brains. I think the men who committed the robbery or helped with the robbery were all amateurs. Take Tarry Joe—Joe Briggs—for instance. Reputation as being a hard worker. Previous conviction didn't come to light until we started checking up on everyone. I was willing to bet that the rest, whoever they were, had never committed any crime before. I think, apart from Briggs, that they all went off to their homes and lived blameless lives until they felt it was safe. No one wanted to know what I thought, though. They all said that amateurs would have betrayed themselves by now.

"I even went out to Spain, to Benidorm, to talk to Briggs. But his criminal associates must have tipped him off, because he had disappeared. He surfaced again, from all reports, after I had left. You're not going to play amateur detective, are you?"

"I was just interested in getting all the facts for my book," said Fell.

"I don't want to depress you," said Mr. Rudfern, "but that first book never sold much and who's going to be interested in a second book?"

"I can try," said Fell stubbornly.

"Let me give you a bit of advice. It's no use raking over the past. Facts don't come to the surface, but mud does. You could inadvertently hurt a lot of people. There were a lot of wild accusations flying around at the time."

"I'll let you know how we're getting on," said Fell.

"Don't. I'm an old man now and don't want to be bothered." Mr. Rudfern picked up a small brass bell from the table beside him and rang it. The door opened promptly and his daughter appeared immediately, as if she had been waiting outside. "See them out," said Mr. Rudfern.

He leaned back and closed his eyes. The interview was over.

"What did you make of that?" exclaimed Maggie. "He was warning you off, wasn't he?"

"He probably doesn't want anyone finding out who did it when he couldn't," said Fell. "You know, I've been thinking.

What about going round to the offices of the local paper? Maybe someone there can put us in touch with a reporter or someone who's still alive who reported on the case?"

"Good idea." Maggie started the car and they set off for the High Street, where the offices of the *Buss Courier* were situated.

After explaining what they wanted to a power-dressed receptionist with mandarin-long fingernails who looked as if she believed she was meant for better things, they were told to wait. Grey light shone into the reception area through a large plate-glass window. A newspaper performed an erratic ballet down the street outside and then, after a final entrechat, sailed up over the roofs and disappeared. They were seated side by side on a tweed sofa. In front of them was a low black coffee table, chipped and scarred. A cheese plant was slowly dying in one corner. There were framed front pages of the *Buss Courier* on the lemon-painted walls.

"Excuse me," said the receptionist, making them jump, so absorbed had both of them been in their own thoughts—Fell's in worries about the money and Maggie's in worries about Fell.

"The editor will see you now. Jessie will show you the way." A shy thin girl had emerged from a side door and stood waiting.

They followed Jessie up a narrow flight of stairs, across the reporters' room, to a frosted glass door which bore the legend. "T. J. Whittaker, Editor."

Jessie opened the door and ushered them in. The editor rose to meet them. He was a red-faced, fleshy man with a beer gut hanging over baggy trousers. His striped shirt was open at the neck. He had beetling eyebrows under which his heavy face sagged down.

"Sit down," he said. "So you're writing a book on our train robbery. I was a reporter on that case. Dolphin, hey? That was the name of the signalman."

"My father," said Fell. "I only just discovered he was a suspect."

"Why? I thought you would have grown up on stories of it."

"No, he never mentioned it."

"So what do you want to write a book about it for?"

Fell decided to take the plunge. "I am really trying to prove my father's innocence. He was pulled in for questioning."

"But he wasn't charged," said Mr. Whittaker.

"Still . . . I've been to see Inspector Rudfern."

"Oh, really? I never found him much help at any time. Anyway, I'd better tell you what I know, seeing as it's a quiet day. I was a reporter then and—"

The door to his office burst unceremoniously open and a young reporter said, "We've got a murder, Mr. Whittaker."

The editor stood up and lifted his jacket from the back of his chair.

"Where? Who?" he demanded.

"Down at the Railway Tavern. A knifing. Landlord says the chap was called Andy Briggs."

FOUR

†

FELL and Maggie made their way slowly out of the newspaper offices. When they were outside, Maggie said, "I'm glad he's dead. But what's worrying me is that whoever killed him might have something to do with the robbery and come looking for us."

"Let's just hope it was a drunken brawl," said Fell. "I'm tired. Let's go home and go to bed."

And I wish that were an invitation, thought Maggie gloomily once again. They seemed to be moving deeper into a nightmare. If only they could get through it together, really together.

She drove them home. As she climbed the stairs to the bedroom, she heard the phone ring. "Could you answer that, Maggie?" called Fell. "I can't take any more today."

Maggie ran downstairs and picked up the phone. "Melissa here," breathed the voice at the other end.

"I'll get Fell," said Maggie wearily.

"No, it's about next Wednesday. I've invited Fell to dinner and I forgot to tell him to bring you. Are you free?"

"Yes, thank you," said Maggie. "What time?"

"Eight o'clock, and I forgot to give Fell the address. It's number 5, Malvern Lane."

"Thank you," said Maggie again. "Very kind of you."

"See you both then. 'Byee!"

"Who was it?" called Fell from his bedroom as he heard Maggie mounting the stairs again.

"Melissa."

He shot out of his bedroom and confronted Maggie on the landing. "Is she still on the phone?"

"No, she called to invite me to dinner as well."

She averted her eyes quickly, but not before she had seen the look of dismay on Fell's face.

"How kind of her," he said bleakly.

"You're disappointed," said Maggie. "I'll tell her I've got a headache and can't go."

Fell looked at her hopefully and then his mouth drooped at the corners. "She would think it odd if you don't come."

"Like I said, I could make an excuse."

"No, she's probably not interested in me anyway. How could she be?"

Maggie wanted to shout out that any woman with half a brain would be interested in Fell, but kept quiet. Perhaps it would be better to go after all and study the enemy at close quarters. "Let's get some sleep," she said instead.

Fell rushed out the next morning to buy the local paper. The murder was on the front page. A man, said the report, was helping police with their inquiries.

“I want to know who this man is,” said Fell, after reading the paper.

“We could go back and ask that editor,” suggested Maggie. “Gosh, it’s so hot already. Your dandelion summer’s come back.”

Maggie was wearing a cool sky-blue cotton dress. The days when she felt she could breakfast in a dressing gown were over. She never confronted Fell in the mornings without being fully dressed and made up. “I’ll make us some breakfast and then we’ll go,” she said, moving towards the kitchen.

“Only toast for me,” Fell called after her. “I couldn’t eat a full breakfast.”

They set out half an hour later, walking in the blinding sunshine. The air was close and humid. Outside the newspaper offices, Fell, who had been carrying his jacket over his arm, put it on.

The bored receptionist, to their request, said that Mr. Whittaker was at the court. “Not far,” said Fell. “Let’s walk round there and see if we can find him.”

As they approached the Georgian courthouse in the centre of the town, they saw the portly figure of the editor. He was talking to a young woman. They stood a little way off, summoning up the courage to interrupt his conversation, when he turned and saw them. He said goodbye to the woman and hailed them with, “Sorry I had to dash off the other day. Got time for a drink?”

Fell looked at his watch. It was quarter to ten in the morning. “Bit early. They won’t be open yet.”

“Follow me. They’re always open for Tommy Whittaker.”

He marched up to the doors of a pub called the Red Lion. The pub was an old Tudor building, black and white and leaning so crazily towards the street, it seemed a miracle it hadn't fallen over like some of its drunken customers. Tommy Whittaker rapped loudly on the door, which opened a crack. "Oh, it's you," said the landlord grumpily. "You may as well come in."

"What'll you have?" asked Tommy.

"Orange juice," said Maggie, and Fell said he would have the same.

"Nonsense; have a real drink."

Intimidated by his overbearing manner, Fell changed his order to a gin and tonic, and Maggie weakly said she would have the same. The landlord said ungraciously that he hadn't any ice.

"I'm surprised he let you in," said Fell as Tommy downed a large whisky and then attacked a pint of beer.

"He knows what's good for him," said Tommy. "The newspaper runs a Best Pub of the Year Award."

"I shouldn't think this place would qualify," said Fell, looking around. Like a lot of English pubs which looked charming and quaint on the outside, the inside was a disappointment. A fruit machine flickered in one corner. The floor was covered in green linoleum, scarred with cigarette burns. The ceiling between the low beams, which had once been white, was now yellow with nicotine. Some of the tables still had dirty glasses on them from the night before.

"No, but he lives in hope."

"What we wanted to ask you," said Fell, squeezing his hands together, "is about the murder of Andy Briggs."

"Oh, that. No great mystery there. Drunken fight."

"Was the man who killed Andy connected with the railway?"

Tommy laughed and took another pull at his pint. "You're a conspiracy theorist. Bet you're one of those ones who surf the Internet trying to find out if the American government is hiding aliens from us."

"I haven't even got a computer," said Fell defensively.

"If you're writing a book, you'd better get one and take one giant leap into the twenty-first century. Where was I?"

He drained his glass of beer. "Ready for another?"

"I'll get them." Fell ordered a pint and a double whisky for Tommy and another gin and tonic for himself and Maggie.

"Thanks," said Tommy, loosening his tie when Fell returned to the table with the drinks. "God, it's hot. Drink up."

Fell and Maggie obediently gulped down their first gin and tonic and started on the second.

"So who have the police got for the murder of Andy Briggs?" asked Fell.

"Pete Murphy, out-of-work villain. He picked a fight with Briggs. Murphy's a small ratlike creature. Briggs is a big chap, or was, rather. So Briggs tells him to come outside and is ready to beat the sh—— the life out of him. Pete pulls a knife and sinks it into Briggs. Surrounded by witnesses at the time, because everyone had followed them out of the pub to watch the fight. They all jump on Pete and sit on him until the police arrive. End of story."

Maggie and Fell exchanged brief, happy looks of relief. Nothing to do with the robbery. No villain to come looking for them.

"So how are you getting on with the robbery?" asked Tommy.

"Not very far," said Fell. "I would like to clear my father's name. Do you know where Terry Weal lives?"

"I wouldn't bother with him."

"Why?"

"He's a bit crazy. He lives just out of town, near the railway. Before you get to the station, halfway over the bridge, there's a lane off to the right. He lives down there, second cottage from the end."

"We'll try anyway," said Fell. "Can you remember much about the robbery?"

"Course I can. I was a reporter covering it. Well, let me see . . . What is it?" An office boy had come into the pub and right up to Tommy.

"Lady Fleaming's in the office."

"Oh, blimey!" Tommy got to his feet. "She's the proprietor. See you!"

"We'll get this story one of these years," said Fell. "I'm not used to drinking this early in the day. But what a relief Andy's gone and his death is nothing to do with us."

"Have you thought of getting a dishwasher?" Maggie asked.

"You mean a dishwashing machine?"

"Yes."

"Why on earth?"

"I struck Andy on the head with that rolling pin. Even though he died of a knife wound, there'll be an autopsy and they'll start wondering about that blow to the head. What if I caused brain damage? What if the autopsy proves that the stabbing didn't actually kill him but some sort of brain haemorrhage?"

"Okay, but what's that got to do with a dishwasher?"

"They're so clever with forensics these days. I washed and scrubbed that rolling pin. But a dishwasher would really clean it."

"You're worrying too much, Maggie. How could they possibly know he was hit with a rolling pin, of all things? And how could it be connected to us?"

"He may have told someone."

"Let's hope he didn't. I don't even want to consider that," said Fell. "We can throw out the rolling pin if you're really worried. Meanwhile, let's go and see Terry Weal."

They walked out into a wall of heat. "Shall I get the car?" asked Maggie.

"No, let's walk. I'm not used to drinking this early and a walk would clear my head."

They set out in the direction of the station, keeping in the shade of the buildings. But once they crossed the Mayor Bridge which spanned the river, the buildings became low bungalows with long gardens in front, the shade disappeared and the sun struck down fiercely.

"This was a bad idea," mourned Fell. "I should have let you get the car. Do you think it's global warming?"

"I sometimes wonder if it's us, humans, who cause it," said Maggie, taking out a handkerchief and patting her damp face. "Every year, more and more people, and imagine them all sweating like us."

"Not far to go now," said Fell. He remembered walking this way with his mother. That was the time he had been off school with mumps. His mother often took lunch to his father. Sometimes he just ate sandwiches, but mostly he liked hot soup in a thermos flask taken to him. He claimed the thermos never kept the soup hot enough for lunchtime if he took it with him in the morning. Fell wrinkled his brow trying to remember if he and his mother had ever talked about anything on these walks, but all he could remember was her saying, "Don't scuff your feet. Straighten your jacket. Don't slouch." Things like that.

Ahead lay the railway bridge. The day of steam trains was

long gone and yet the air around the station always seemed to smell of soot and cinders.

Halfway across the railway bridge, they turned off to the right and down a lane leading to a row of cottages which had been built in the last century for the railway workers. Most of the cottages had been smartened up and the land between the cottages and the railway line turned into extended gardens. But the second cottage, where they had been told Terry Weal lived, had a forlorn air. The window frames had not been painted in years and the garden gate was hanging off its hinges.

Fell hesitated outside the gate. "I wish we had taken the day off from all this, Maggie."

"May as well go through with it now we're here. We'll take tomorrow off." Maggie held open the gate. "Come on. He can't eat us."

Maggie felt a little pang as she said those words. It was so easy for the two of them to be brave, one encouraging the other. If only they could be a *real* couple.

They walked up a short path made of the same red bricks as the house. There wasn't a bell. The paint on the door was blistered.

Fell knocked at the door. He heard the signal at the station clanking down. A train was coming. It would be the down train to London, he thought, looking at his watch. The signal went down ten minutes before the train arrived.

The door opened and a small bent man who smelt peculiarly of ham soup stared at them. "What d'ye want? I'm not buying anything."

"We're not selling anything. I'm Fell Dolphin."

"Dolphin's boy? I've nothing to say to you."

"Why?" asked Maggie.

"Because I know Dolphin was in on that robbery, that's why."

"But it was a coincidence that you were ill that day," cried Fell.

"I wasn't ill. Dolphin says, says he, that he wanted to take the Saturday off instead. They didn't like us switching shifts unless we were ill. He said he'd give me ten pounds to say I was ill. I told the police that. But he got away with it. Now he's dead. They didn't get him." The old man spat somewhere at the region of Fell's feet. "Why are you bothering me?"

"I want to clear my father's name."

"That's a joke."

"I'm writing a book."

"Well, put this in your book. Your father was a criminal!" He slammed the door in their faces.

They heard the approaching roar of the train. Fell seized Maggie's hand. "Come on."

"Where are we going?" gasped Maggie as he pulled her down the path.

"London!" cried Fell. "I'm sick of all this and I've never been to London. Have you?"

But Maggie's reply was drowned by the roar of the approaching train. They sprinted to the station and collapsed panting in a first-class compartment.

"Have you been to London before?" demanded Fell again.

"No," said Maggie. "Never."

"Isn't it odd?" said Fell. "Here we are living an hour and a half's train ride from London and yet none of us has ever seen the place."

The ticket collector came round and Fell explained they hadn't had time to buy tickets at the station.

"Have you enough money on you?" asked Maggie.

"Yes, I've got plenty. I've got this habit of carrying a wad of notes around with me. Damn that horrible old man, Maggie. There was a ring of truth about what he said. And why should he lie?"

"Spite?"

"No, I don't think so. We must find someone else who might tell us why my father found it so important to get that Saturday off."

"Surely Inspector Rudfern would remember."

"We'll try him again. In the meantime, let's have a holiday."

Lunch was announced in the dining car, so they went along and enjoyed the novelty of eating while the sunny countryside slipped smoothly past.

"I've just thought of something," said Maggie.

"What?" asked Fell, turning dreamy eyes from the countryside.

"Those twenty-pound notes in the cash box."

Fell's eyes sharpened and focused on her. "What about them?"

"I just remembered. They're current issue. If they were part of the robbery, then the notes would be old. I mean, I think the twenty-pound note has changed at least a couple of times since the robbery."

"That would mean," said Fell slowly, "that the money didn't come from the robbery."

"Unless, of course, one of your parents changed the notes. They're pretty crisp and new."

Fell shook his head in bewilderment. "This is my parents you're talking about, Maggie. You have no idea how strict and moralizing they were. I cannot imagine either of them doing anything criminal."

"If they came by the money honestly but wanted to avoid paying tax on it, your mother, say, might just have gone from bank to bank changing just a certain amount. Did she ever go away?"

Fell was about to shake his head, but then he remembered she had gone away for two weeks just a few years ago. "She went on a bus tour," he said, "for a fortnight. I remember looking forward to two weeks of freedom." But she had phoned every day, to the hotel where he was working or to the house, with instructions to do that or clean this, and so he had never enjoyed any of his brief freedom. He had an odd but vivid picture of his mother going from town to town and bank to bank doggedly changing the twenty-pound notes for new ones.

"Let's stop worrying just for today," urged Fell. He sank back in his seat and soon there was a dreamy smile on his face. Maggie felt some of her pleasure in the day fading. She was sure Fell was dreaming about their forthcoming visit to Melissa.

They alighted at Paddington Station. "Now where?" asked Maggie.

"We'll take a taxi and look at the sights."

They ran up enormous taxi bills going round the sights from Buckingham Palace to the Tower and St. Paul's Cathedral. The final taxi deposited them at Piccadilly Circus where they stood like two children, looking round. Fell bought a street map and suggested they walk to Covent Garden. "I once read a book where it mentioned an old restaurant called Rules. It's supposed to be the oldest restaurant in London."

Maggie had forgotten about the robbery, about Melissa. All she was aware of was the glory of walking through the summer London streets with Fell.

In Covent Garden, they walked through the chattering crowds and turned in to Maiden Lane. "There it is," said Fell.

"I wish I had dressed up," said Maggie, suddenly nervous. She was wearing a blue cotton dress and Fell was in an open-necked shirt and jeans. "It's the tourist season," said Fell. "They'll be used to people dressing casually."

The woman at the desk smiled at them, and said they were lucky. A cancellation had just come in. She led them to a table, smiled at them again and handed them large menus. Maggie looked around at the gleaming brass and mahogany and at all the oil paintings on the walls.

"I read that King Edward the Seventh used to bring his mistresses here," said Fell. "He had a special staircase built to the rooms above so he could sneak them in."

The food turned out to be of the stick-to-your-ribs variety and beautifully cooked. They talked and talked, swapping reminiscences about their working days at the Palace Hotel, drinking wine and chattering away.

Finally Fell called for the bill. The waiter smiled down at them as he took Fell's payment and generous tip. "On your honeymoon, sir?" he asked.

"No," said Fell. "Let's go, Maggie."

They walked down to the Strand and caught a cab to Paddington Station. As they swung round Trafalgar Square, Maggie looked out at the lions at the base of Nelson's Column and wished with all her heart that they really were on their honeymoon. But it had been a day to remember, and the Maggies of this world took such days as they came and photographed them in their minds and pasted them in the mental photo album to take out and look at when the days were dark.

The last train to Buss had gone, so they took a train to Worcester and a taxi from there to Buss.

"Must remember we're going to Melissa's tomorrow," said Fell as he unlocked the door.

How could I ever forget, thought Maggie. Damn the woman!

Fell said the following day that he wanted to go out on his own to do some shopping. Maggie guessed that he would be nervously looking to see if he could find anything better to wear than he had got for the all-important evening ahead.

To soothe her feelings, she decided to bake a tray of small sponge cakes. She had not baked anything since her teens. She opened a cookery book she had bought recently and set to work.

Fell arrived back after an hour, empty-handed. He had cruised the shops but had decided at last to wear his new suit. To buy yet another suit seemed indecent. Habits of thrift die hard.

"Nice smell," he said, walking into the kitchen.

"I'm trying my hand at some sponge cakes," said Maggie. "They're nearly ready. Isn't that someone at the door?"

Fell went to answer it. Two young men stood on the doorstep, one lugging a camera bag. *"Buss Courier,"* said one cheerfully. "I'm Peter South and this is my photographer, Derek."

"What's happened?" asked Fell nervously.

"Nothing drastic. Our editor said you were looking into the old train robbery and were hoping to write a book about it." Peter eyed Fell shrewdly. He felt sure if he told Fell the truth, that it was a quiet time for news and that the editor had asked him to see if there was a story in Fell's investigations, this nervous man might back off, so he said, "Our editor took a fancy to you and thought you might like some help in your research."

"Come in," said Fell.

They both walked into the living room. The cameraman put his bag on the floor, opened it and began to take out camera and lenses. "What's all that for?" asked Fell.

"Just a photograph for our files," said Peter soothingly.

Maggie came in from the kitchen. Fell introduced the newspapermen and explained the reason for their visit.

"I've just made some sponge cakes," said Maggie. "Would you like some?"

"Love some," said Peter, smiling at Maggie. She smiled back, liking his round, pleasant face and mop of curly hair.

"Now," said Peter, turning to Fell, "you'd better tell me how far you've got."

Fell gave him a carefully edited story, omitting the visit of Andy Briggs and the mysterious money in the cash box. Maggie came in with a tray and passed round sponge cakes and tea.

"I say," said Peter enthusiastically, "these are as light as a feather." He beamed at Maggie, liking what he saw. Peter's dream was of finding a nice girl to look after him. He loved the fact that Maggie's newly slim figure was wrapped in a flowery apron. He hadn't thought women wore aprons any more. He liked her shiny hair in its feathery cut and the wide-eyed friendly look of her large green eyes behind the thick glasses.

"You two are engaged, right?" he asked.

"Er, um, yes," said Fell reluctantly and a shadow crossed Maggie's expressive eyes.

Oho, what's this? thought Peter. And at least they're not married. Wonder if Maggie might meet me sometime for a drink?

He ate three of the sponge cakes and then said, "Now, if you two would like to pose for pictures."

"Why?" asked Maggie sharply.

"Just for the file. Like I told Fell here, it's a quiet day and our editor's taken a fancy to you and thinks I might be able to help you with your research."

"Oh, in that case . . . Is it all right if I take off my glasses?"

"Go ahead," said Peter. Maggie removed her glasses. She blinked a little, looking feminine and vulnerable.

Fell and Maggie stood side by side while the photographer, Derek, banged off several pictures.

"I think that wraps it up," said Peter cheerfully. "I'll start off by going through the old newspaper files and I'll copy anything I think you might have missed and bring it round."

"That's very good of you," said Fell.

"Here's my card." But Peter handed it to Maggie.

Fell ushered them outside into the sunlight. "Forgot something," said Peter and dived back into the house, leaving Fell standing outside with the photographer.

Maggie was clearing away the teacups. "Any chance of meeting me one evening for a drink?" asked Peter.

"Maybe," said Maggie.

"Well, you've got my card. Phone me if you're free."

When he had gone, Maggie stood, blinking in surprise. How odd. He knew she was engaged and yet he had asked her out. She should have reminded him sharply that she *was* engaged. But she wasn't really, and there was Melissa, after all.

†

That evening, after having tried on about everything in her wardrobe, Maggie dismally decided to settle for comfort rather than style. She felt she could not possibly compete with Melissa, no matter what she wore. She settled on a green silk blouse and a long black velvet skirt. The velvet was worn in places at the back of the skirt, so she steamed it with the iron and convinced herself that the worn places no longer showed.

There was a dark pit inside her as they both got into her little car. Fell seemed to be lit up from within. "What a beautiful evening," he sighed.

"It hasn't started yet," said Maggie sourly, letting in the clutch.

Fell was silent on the short drive to Melissa's house, but out of the corner of her eye Maggie saw the nervous clasping and unclasping of his long fingers.

They parked in front of Melissa's house. "What a beautiful place!" exclaimed Fell.

"It's just a villa like the one Rudfern lives in," said Maggie. "Come along, Fell, and don't stand there gawping."

"You would think we had been married for years," snapped Fell, and Maggie felt close to tears.

When Melissa opened the door to them, Maggie, who had thought it could not be possible to feel any more miserable, found that, yes, it was indeed possible. Melissa was wearing a slinky black silk trouser suit and her face was expertly made up.

Melissa led the way into a sitting room. Maggie glanced quickly around. It looked as if it had been put together by a professional interior designer, but some time ago, when dried flowers and shades of brown and cream had been all the rage.

One again, Maggie felt sure Melissa was after Fell's money. Melissa lifted a bottle out of an ice bucket on a sideboard and wrapped it in a white cloth. "I thought we would have some vintage champagne," she said. She poured out three glasses and handed one each to Fell and Maggie.

Maggie took a sip and her eyebrows raised. Working at the Palace Hotel had given her a knowledge of wine, and she was suddenly sure that what she was drinking was certainly not vintage champagne.

"It is hot," Melissa was saying. "Let's carry our drinks out into the garden." She smiled at Fell and led him towards the open french windows.

Maggie followed, deliberately leaving her handbag behind. As they were about to sit down in white garden chairs in front of a white wrought-iron table, Maggie said, "I've left my handbag. Excuse me a moment."

She walked swiftly into the sitting room and picked up her handbag. Then she veered slightly to the left, to the sideboard, out of sight of Melissa and twitched back the cloth covering the bottle. Effervescent cider! Cheapskate.

Maggie joined Fell and Melissa just in time to hear Fell saying, "This is very good champagne."

Fool, thought Maggie. Wait until I tell him. And then realized that was something she must not do. Fell would simply accuse her of spying again.

As she joined them, she noticed Melissa had a hand on Fell's knee and was saying, "Have you thought any more about my little business proposition?"

"I've been a bit taken up with other matters," said Fell, "but it does seem a good idea. Don't you think so, Maggie?"

"Yes," said Maggie with well-manufactured enthusiasm.

"Fell and I are a bit naïve about business, Melissa, so we'll probably discuss the matter with the lawyer and bank manager—you know, get them to evaluate the profits of your business and all that."

For one moment, Maggie and Melissa locked eyes. Then Melissa said with a light laugh, "Oh, we're friends, aren't we? We don't need to be fussed with all that sort of stuff."

"No, not at all," said Fell, who couldn't take his eyes off her.

Over dinner, Melissa chattered on, telling stories about people who came into the shop, discussing alternative medicine, and Fell hung on every word like a man bewitched. The table was bathed in soft candlelight. The sitting room had been lit by two lamps. Maggie wanted Fell to see Melissa in a strong light so that he would realize just how old she was. She gave her handbag, which she had placed open at her feet, a hard kick. "Oh," said Maggie, "I've upset my bag and I keep everything in there. No, don't move. I'll pick the things up." She moved quickly to the light switch and snapped it on. Before she bent to retrieve her belongings, she had a glimpse of Melissa's face, cruelly exposed in the overhead light. Surely Fell would notice the pouches under the eyes, the grooves down the sides of the mouth, the wrinkles on the upper lip? But as soon as she had stuffed everything back into her bag, Melissa rose with one fluid movement and switched the light off. In the candlelight, Maggie noticed that Fell's eyes were as adoring as ever. Fell saw only what he wanted to see.

Maggie began to talk about a book she had just read, recounting some of the more amusing scenes. She talked well, but Fell did not listen. He only wished with all his heart that he were alone with Melissa. He had a longing to tell her that he was not really engaged to Maggie.

His moment came after dinner, when Melissa asked him to help her stack the dishwasher and told Maggie that one helping her was enough and Maggie could go out to the garden and relax.

As Maggie sat in the garden, Melissa's voice came faintly to her ears, accompanied by Fell's amused laugh.

Fell was battling with himself. He longed to tell Melissa that he was not really engaged and yet loyalty to Maggie held him back. He could not really tell Melissa anything like that until he had discussed it with Maggie first. Then Melissa gave him an intimate smile and said, "I don't think your little friend trusts me."

"Maggie? Why?"

"All that talk about bankers and lawyers."

"She had no right to say that. It's my money."

"Perhaps we really ought to discuss it on our own."

"That would be better," said Fell, his senses quickening at the thought of having a date with Melissa. With such a woman on his arm, he'd be the envy of every man in Buss.

"Why don't I take you for dinner to that French restaurant on Friday," he said.

"Good idea. What time?"

"Eight o'clock."

Her eyes caressed him. "I'll see you there."

When they joined Maggie in the garden, Maggie's radar picked up that they must have come to some arrangement that did not include her, for Melissa now seemed anxious to be rid of them. She pointedly yawned several times and Maggie said, "You do need your beauty sleep."

"Don't I just," laughed Melissa, ignoring the sarcastic edge in Maggie's voice.

†

They got into the car outside. There was not a breath of air. "We need a thunderstorm," said Maggie.

Fell stared straight ahead for a moment, then he said, "You know, Maggie, I don't think there's really any need to bring in lawyers and accountants if I want to go into business with Melissa."

"Why?"

"Well." Fell gave an awkard laugh. "You can tell she's got money and that means she must have a flourishing business."

"How do you mean, you can see she's got money?"

"It's a big house and expensively furnished and then she went to the trouble to serve vintage champagne."

All Maggie's good resolutions to go carefully on the subject of Melissa vanished in a wave of jealousy.

"That wasn't vintage champagne, for a start," she said. "It was effervescent cider."

"Nonsense."

"I looked at the label, Fell."

"You were spying!"

"No, I thought it didn't taste like vintage champagne, so I had a look. And the furnishings were expensive years ago, all that brown and cream."

"It is just as well I am meeting Melissa on her own for dinner on Friday," snapped Fell. "How can I keep a clear mind on the subject when you're always snooping and spying?"

"That's unfair!"

They went into the house in stony silence. Maggie went up

to her room, her face flaming. She sat down on the edge of her bed. Now she'd done it. Fell had not asked her to leave, but he might in the morning. She would need to do something to heal the breach. She washed and undressed, but sleep would not come. Even with the window wide open, the bedroom was hot and stifling. Her feet throbbed and ached. Out of her small savings she had bought a new pair of high heels to wear that evening. They were very high indeed. Suffering for vanity, she thought, punching the pillow, which suddenly seemed to have become as hard as a brick. If only she could think of something to restore herself to favour. Something about the robbery. She was just falling asleep when an idea struck her. Fell, Fellworth Dolphin. The couple in the garden in front of the big house. What if they had named him after the *house?* Maggie resolved to go straight to the library in the morning.

The next morning when she went downstairs, it was to find a curt note for her placed on top of the electric kettle, saying, "Gone for a walk, Fell."

Maggie looked at the clock. Only nine and the library did not open until ten. She decided to go out somewhere and have breakfast. She did not want to risk another quarrel with Fell.

As she walked off down the street in the direction of the centre of the town, the close heat of the day surrounded her, an exhausted heat redolent of car fumes. The sky above was covered in a milky haze. A few dried leaves, loosened by the hot summer, fell down from the plane trees on the street and dropped wearily onto the ground at her feet as if the very leaves, like the people of Buss, had become exhausted by this odd, seemingly never-ending dandelion summer.

She went into a café for coffee and a croissant and watched the population of Buss walk slowly by. No one wanted to hurry in this heat.

When she had finished her light breakfast, she walked to the library. She found a section with books on country houses in Worcestershire, took several out and sat down to look though them. No Fellworth. And yet, if there was some connection between the railway station and the couple on the photograph, it figured that one of them might have used the station. Then she thought, the Gloucestershire border is close. She returned the books and took out three on houses in Gloucestershire. In a small battered volume, in the index, the name "Fellworth" seemed to leap up at her out of the page. She turned to the item in the book. It was only a small paragraph. No photo. "Fellworth Manor," it said, "is an undistinguished Victorian manor house, rebuilt on the site of the original Elizabethan manor house in 1895. Even at that time, the destruction of the old manor roused public feeling, but the Fellworth family claimed they wanted a more convenient modern building. Situated near the village of Ablington outside Cirencester."

Maggie felt triumphant. Here indeed was news to take Fell's mind off Melissa. She had the relevant page photocopied and hurried home.

Fell was watering the garden, the spray from the hose setting rainbows to dance over the flowers. The "grave" meant for Andy Briggs had been filled in.

She ignored the hostile look in his eyes and waved the photocopy at him. "Look what I've found."

Fell took the paper from her. His hostility fled and his eyes lit up. "How on earth did you get this, Maggie?"

Maggie told him of her brainwave. "Let's go now," she urged.

Soon they had locked up and were in the car heading towards Gloucestershire.

"Isn't there any air-conditioning in this thing?" asked Fell.

"Too old, too cheap and too British," said Maggie. "What happened to your driving lessons, Fell? I thought you had booked up for a crash course."

"I put the lessons off for a bit," said Fell. "With all this business about the robbery, I didn't feel I could cope with driving lessons."

"I could teach you," said Maggie.

"No," said Fell hurriedly. "I paid for the lessons in advance, so I may as well take them."

He had been dreaming all night of disengaging himself from Maggie so that he could tell Melissa he was free.

Maggie sensed his withdrawal from her. She cursed herself for having been so clumsy as to attack Melissa. Then she remembered that reporter, Peter South. She would phone him and ask him if he was free on Friday. Then she would tell Fell she had a date. If Fell realized she wasn't holding on to him, they would be at ease with each other again, and surely she could find some way of exposing Melissa.

They had to stop several times to ask for directions to Fellworth Manor, which seemed to be buried somewhere along a network of country lanes. At last they reached the gates of the manor house. Fell got out and swung them open, and Maggie drove through. When he got back in the car, he found his heart was beating hard.

Maggie drove slowly up the long drive under a long arch

of wilting trees. Everything drooped in the heat. And then the house came into view.

"It's the right house," said Maggie. "The one in your photo."

It was a Victorian mansion built of an ugly combination of red brick and yellowish Bath stone. It had mullioned windows reflecting the Victorian love affair with things medieval. But it was very large and imposing for all that, and as Maggie parked and Fell got out of the car, he could feel his knees trembling.

"Well, here goes, Maggie," he said, and squaring his shoulders, he walked up to the door.

FIVE

†

FELL waited patiently, with Maggie behind him. The whole countryside was wrapped in a hot, sleepy hush. A vision of his parents' modest home rose before his eyes. They could not possibly have any connection with such a place as this.

The door was opened by a middle-aged woman in a blue uniform with a white collar and cuffs.

"Are you the owner?" asked Fell.

"No, I am Mrs. Wakeham's nurse."

"May I see her?"

"Does she know you? Do you have an appointment?"

"No. My name is Fellworth Dolphin. I think Mrs. Wakeham might have known my parents."

"Wait here."

She shut the door, and he could hear the heels of her sensible black lace-up shoes clacking off into the distance.

Fell was wearing his best suit. He wished he could remove

his jacket. He could feel stains of sweat spreading under his armpits. He suddenly wished Melissa were with him, not Maggie, Melissa with her sophistication and elegance. He glanced at Maggie. Her hair had gone limp in the heat and her face was shiny.

The door opened again. "Mrs. Wakeham will see you for a few moments," said the nurse. "Follow me."

They followed her through a house which seemed to contain too much furniture, too many oil paintings, too many objets d'art. It was cooler than outside, but the rooms through which she led them had a musty smell, as if no one had lived in them for a long while.

They followed the nurse out into the garden at the back. An elderly lady sat at a table under a cedar tree.

"Mr. Dolphin," announced the nurse, "and . . . ?"

"Miss Partlett, Maggie Partlett, Fell's fiancée."

Oh, I must stop this charade, thought Fell miserably. I don't want to be engaged to this girl with the shiny face and limp hair.

"Sit down," commanded Mrs. Wakeham. She had a surprisingly deep voice.

They both sat on wrought-iron chairs facing her.

"I regret to say I have never heard of you," said Mrs. Wakeham. "That will be all, Martha."

"Shall I bring some tea or lemonade?" asked the nurse.

"No, they will not be staying long."

The nurse went back into the house. Fell studied Mrs. Wakeham, and Mrs. Wakeham studied Fell. She had a heavy, patrician-nosed face under the shade of a straw hat. Her eyes were of a washed-out blue. She had a dowager's hump and despite the heat of the day was wearing a woollen cardigan over a tailored blouse and skirt.

"I believe you have some mistaken belief that I knew your parents," she said.

"It's because of my name," said Fell, who was beginning to feel ridiculous under that pale gaze. "I've always wondered why I was called Fellworth. I saw the name of the house and that made me wonder."

"But your parents may have seen the name of the house in a book or when they were passing by the gates," said Mrs. Wakeham. "Did you not think of that?"

"I am sorry for wasting your time." Fell just wanted to get away. "You see, I had this crazy idea I might have been adopted. So . . . if you will excuse us . . ." He half-rose to his feet.

"Sit down," said Mrs. Wakeham, "and take your jacket off. Old women like me do not feel the heat. I am curious. Why should you believe you were adopted?"

"Because I cannot remember any parental love. Because my parents left me an awful lot of money."

"So you did not come here to try to get money out of me?"

Fell stared at her, first in shock and then in dawning anger. "Of course not!"

She studied him closely. "But you had a good education?"

"I attended Buss Comprehensive, but could not go to university because I had to support my parents. Until my mother's recent death, I worked as a waiter at the Palace Hotel."

She leaned back in her chair and murmured, "But they were paid well for your education."

Maggie let out a little gasp.

"The money," said Fell slowly. "That money I found. That was from you. Why?"

There was a long silence. A small plane droned overhead. A bird in the heavy branches above them gave a dusty cheep.

"I thought you had come here for money," said Mrs. Wakeham. "I may as well tell you. There is no reason why I should not tell you. First we will have tea."

She rang a little bell on the table and when the nurse appeared, said, "We will have tea after all, Martha." After the nurse had gone, Mrs. Wakeham raised a wrinkled hand. "We will wait for tea before I tell you anything." She turned her gaze on Maggie. "And so you are engaged to Mr. Dolphin?"

"Yes. I am Fell's fiancée. We met while we were both working at the hotel."

"You have fine eyes and a kind face. I am pleased. Tell me about yourself."

Maggie began to talk about what it had been like being a waitress. She told several funny stories about the customers and Mrs. Wakeham gave a dry laugh. Fell was amazed that Maggie should be so at ease, so unintimidated.

Tea was served. The nurse retreated again. Mrs. Wakeham took a sip of tea and said, "Now, where shall I begin? At the beginning, I suppose. My son Paul was very wild, but at the time, we did not know much about his wildness. He was studying in the City for his stockbroker exams. He came down here at weekends. He got a local girl pregnant."

"My mother?" asked Fell through dry lips.

She nodded. "She was called Greta Feeney and she was the local barmaid. Paul refused point-blank to marry her. She had respectable parents and Greta did not want an abortion, but she agreed to having the baby adopted if we arranged everything. My husband often took the train from Buss. Dolphin had once told him he regretted that he and his wife could not have children. My husband, Colonel Wakeham, approached him and said he would give him a large sum of money to adopt the baby. Dolphin agreed but said he would only do it for a lump sum in cash. Adoption is difficult and we all wanted to keep the matter quiet. So it was decided just to hand the baby over after it was born. Mrs. Dolphin agreed to fake pregnancy. She came here in the supposed last days of her pregnancy. The baby, you, was subsequently handed over, and that was that. Dolphin agreed to never come near us or approach us again."

"My mother?" asked Fell.

"Greta? I regret to say she died of cancer."

"And my father?"

"How odd to hear you call him that. Paul was persuaded by my husband to join the army. My husband was a retired colonel and thought the British army a cure-all for wayward youth. Paul was posted to Cyprus. He was killed in a drunken brawl." She rang the bell again and when the nurse appeared, said, "Martha, on top of the bookshelves in the morning room, you will find a photo album. Bring it, please."

Fell could feel his heart hammering against his ribs. Orphaned in one stroke on a hot day! And yet gradually, as they waited, he began slowly to relax. All the guilt he had felt over not loving what he had believed to be his parents was ebbing away. And that money had not come from the train robbery! There was no need to bother much any more about who had committed the robbery.

Martha came back and placed a large leather-bound photo album on the table. Again, Mrs. Wakeham waited until the nurse had left. Then she opened the album. She withdrew a photograph and handed it to Fell. Fell looked down at the photograph of a laughing young man. He had a square handsome face, brown hair and bright blue eyes. "I don't look at all like him," he said.

"No, you look like your mother."

"Do you have a photograph of her?"

"I'm afraid not. You must now forget about it. Her parents are dead as well. Greta married a decent man, a local farmer. He knew nothing about you, and I do not want him to know anything. I am glad the Dolphins left you money. It seems to me you have had a hard life. But I assure you, they cheated you. That money was for your upbringing and to give you a good education." She rested her head on her hand. "Now I must ask you to leave. I am tired."

Fell and Maggie stood up. "May we call again?" asked Fell.

"No, it brings back painful memories. I am old. I wish to be left in peace." She rang the bell.

"But I am your grandson!" protested Fell.

"I know. I know. But I do not want to be troubled any more by bad memories. I want to remember only good things about my son. Ah, Martha, please show them out."

Maggie and Fell followed Martha back through a chain of rooms and back out through the front door. They got into the car and Maggie drove off.

"It seems as if no one wants me," said Fell.

"You've got me," said Maggie. "As a friend, I mean."

Fell experienced a sudden rush of affection for her. Solid, dependable Maggie. "Well, it looks as if we don't need to worry about the robbery any more," he said. "So they hid the money, not wanting the tax man to get it. They lived on as little of it as they could. They were misers. And I can't declare it without exposing where I got it from."

Maggie wanted to ask—where do we go from here? She

had a sinking feeling that it was only the investigation about the robbery that was keeping them together. She remembered the reporter, Peter South. She would go out to a phone box and call him and see if he could meet her the following evening. Perhaps if Fell knew someone else was interested in her, he might look at her with new eyes.

Fell was thinking guiltily that he should really do something good for Maggie because shortly he was going to have to tell her that he did not want to pose as her fiancé any more. He said, "Let's go to Oxford."

"All right. Why?"

"I'm going to get you those contact lenses you wanted. There's one of those express opticians in Oxford in the Westgate. And maybe you can pick out a new dress."

And Maggie, not knowing the reason for this sudden generosity, said, "Oh, that's so good of you, Fell."

It was a quiet day at the *Buss Courier.* Peter South lounged back in his office chair, looking at the photo of Maggie and Fell, which had appeared in that day's *Courier* under the bold headline "Signalman's Son Turns Detective to Clear Father's Name." He wondered if Maggie had seen it.

Just then the editor loomed over him. "That French restaurant is very grateful for the good write-up. They've written to say they're offering you a complimentary meal for two. If you can't use the invitation—"

"I can. Thanks," said Peter. The phone on his desk rang. He picked it up as Tommy Whittaker walked away. "This is Maggie, Maggie Partlettt. You may not remember me . . ."

"Course I do," said Peter. "Lot of traffic. Where are you calling from?"

"Oxford. A phone box. I wondered if you would like to meet me tomorrow night?"

"Sure. Tell you what. I'll take you to that French restaurant. Hey, are you still there?"

"Yes, yes, that would be fine. I'll meet you there. What time?"

"Eight. Have you seen . . . ?"

But Maggie had rung off.

The rest of that day, Maggie floated on air. She had her new contact lenses, which she planned to wear for the first time for her date with Peter, and she had also had her hair restyled. As they drove back towards Buss, her bubble of happiness suddenly burst. For a few hours she had forgotten about Melissa. Fell and Melissa would be in the restaurant as well and her evening would be spoilt by watching the rapture in his face.

She parked outside the house. She and Fell got out. Mrs. Moule hobbled to her garden hedge. "If it isn't the famous detectives," she said.

Fell and Maggie stopped still. "What are you talking about?" croaked Fell.

"It's in the paper, the *Buss Courier,*" said Mrs. Moule. "And with a picture, too."

"What about?" asked Maggie.

"All about you trying to clear your father's name."

"Oh, that," said Fell bleakly. All his worries about the robbery came rushing back. "Come along, Maggie," he said. "We'd better go and get a copy."

They walked along to the local newsagent's. They bought a copy of the paper and then stood out on the hot and dusty street and gazed down at the headline. "It was that money," mourned Fell. "Now everyone will think my father really had something to do with it; else why should I talk about clearing his name?"

"We may as well go on with our investigations," said Maggie hopefully—hopeful that any further investigation would keep them together. But Fell shrugged wearily. "I'm tired of the whole thing. You know, Maggie, when you told me about Fellworth Manor, I had this dream I was going to find a family at last. But all I turned out to be was a bastard no one really wanted, not even my mother."

I want you, I need you, I love you. How Maggie would have given anything to be able to say those words, but she knew that Fell in the grip of his obsession would feel trapped and suffocated.

Maggie wondered for the first time whether Fell might not be a virgin. No one could obsess more than a celibate. And surely if he had had physical relationships with women, he would not have fallen so heavily for an older woman.

Back home, they opened all the windows and the kitchen door to let in some air. But the evening was close and hot. The house had a half-finished air. The kitchen was all gleaming and new-looking, but the rest had a temporary air.

"We need some pictures for the walls," said Maggie, looking around the living room. "Those white walls look too naked. And maybe some plants."

"Maybe," said Fell indifferently.

Maggie studied his bent head thoughtfully and then said, "If you're not too tired, we could take a walk down by the river. There might be some air there."

They shut the doors and windows and walked back out into the close heat of evening. "Do you feel like eating?" asked Maggie. "I'm quite hungry."

Fell trudged on, wrapped in his thoughts.

"There's a Chinese restaurant in the High Street," Maggie continued. "We could get a take-out."

"Okay," said Fell listlessly.

People drifted past them in summer clothes, as listless as Fell in the heat, moving like people underwater.

"Oh, look!" said Maggie suddenly. She pointed to the Chinese restaurant, which had a banner outside proclaiming, "Air-Conditioned."

"We'll eat inside," said Maggie. "Fell?"

Fell was standing on the pavement, looking at his feet. She tugged at his arm and then led him inside like a child.

The restaurant was crowded, but a couple was just leaving as they arrived.

As the chill of the air-conditioning surrounded Fell, he suddenly realized he was ravenously hungry.

They ordered the Chef's Special and a bottle of white wine and ate steadily through multiple dishes, at first in silence, and then Fell began to talk again about the robbery. "I suppose we should go on and find out something. It gave me a shock to see that headline. I didn't know they were going to publish anything. That reporter was far from honest with us."

Now was the time to tell Fell that she had a date with "that reporter," but Maggie was too relieved to see him interested and animated once more.

"You spoke about two maintenance workers," she said instead.

"I, what?" Fell pulled his mind out of a dream of marriage to Melissa.

"Two maintenance workers, on the railway," prompted Maggie.

"Oh, them. Fred Flint and Johnny Tremp. I suppose we could start with Tremp. There was a J. Tremp in the phone book." Fell sighed. "Now that we know about the money, I thought we could forget about the whole thing, but that damned reporter has stirred everything up."

"There's one thing I just thought of," said Maggie. "Rudfern said they had kept a close eye on suspects long after the robbery to see if any of them had been spending unusually large sums of money. Surely they would have checked your father's bank account and noticed the lack of withdrawals and wondered what he was living on."

"Yes, that is odd. And yet we can't ask anyone why. I wonder if I should buy a new suit for tomorrow."

"It's your money," said Maggie, lowering her eyes quickly so that he should not see her hate for Melissa in them.

"I've been so used to being thrifty, it seems wicked to spend money on another suit."

"You could compromise. You could buy a new shirt and silk tie."

Fell brightened. "That's a good idea. I want to look my best."

Maggie felt suddenly weary. Perhaps it would be best to forget about Fell altogether.

The next evening, Maggie kept to her room, taking care with her preparations. She somehow could not bring herself to tell Fell she would be in the restaurant at the same time. She carefully put in her new contact lenses and then a soft, leaf green chiffon dress. Maggie had planned to wear this new dress just for Fell, but decided to wear it for Peter. She judged Fell would leave early for the restaurant and so it was. She heard him calling up the stairs, "Bye, Maggie. Don't wait up."

Maggie waited until five to eight and then set out, the chiffon dress fluttering about her legs as she made her way to the restaurant.

It was ten past eight by the time she got there. Peter was standing outside the restaurant, smoking a cigarette.

"You look great," he said, walking forward to meet her. "Do you know Fell's here already with that harpy who runs the health shop?"

"He said something about it. Why do you call her a harpy?"

He took her arm and led her into the restaurant. "Tell you about it."

They were led to one of the best tables by an open window overlooking the terrace and the river.

Maggie saw Fell over in a far corner, talking animatedly to Melissa. After they had ordered their food and Peter had ordered wine, Maggie asked again, "Why do you call her a harpy?"

"Just town gossip. She was warned against starting that business. I mean this is Buss, where the population's idea of health food is fish and chips. So instead to taking advice and selling off the place, she dug her heels in and said she could make it pay. Now she's looking for someone with money. I suppose that's why she's after your fiancé."

"Fell's very attractive," said Maggie loyally.

"Well, I suppose you must think so."

"We were upset by your story, dragging all that stuff up again. You might at least have warned us you were going to write something."

"My boss's idea," said Peter. "Honest."

"Are you sure you didn't ask me out just to find out more?"

Peter smiled at Maggie. "I fancy you rotten, Maggie Partlett."

"Me!"

"I've always wanted to meet a girl with green eyes who wore an apron."

Maggie laughed. "You just want a mother."

"Don't we all. I'm the only man who's honest about it."

Fell heard that familiar laugh and looked across the restaurant. In the candlelight, Maggie's face was glowing and her green eyes shone.

"That reporter again!" he exclaimed.

"What?" Melissa had been in full flow about the benefits of her business.

"Maggie, over there, with that reporter from the *Courier*."

"Well, you're here with me." Melissa threw him a flirtatious look.

"Excuse me." Fell threw down his napkin and walked over to Maggie's table. "What do you think you are doing?" he demanded.

"I'm having dinner with a friend—just like you," said Maggie defensively.

"Your only interest in her is getting another story out of her," Fell accused Peter.

Peter smiled easily. "It may not have dawned on you, but your fiancée is worth any fellow's time. You ain't married yet."

Fell stared at him.

"We'll talk later," said Maggie hurriedly. "Do go back to your dinner, Fell."

Fell looked at her in baffled fury. Then he became aware that the other diners were looking at him curiously. He flushed with embarrassment and went back to Melissa.

"Sorry about that," he mumbled.

"You didn't strike me as the jealous type," teased Melissa.

"I am not jealous. I don't care what Maggie does!"

"Then maybe you shouldn't marry her."

Fell opened his mouth to say he had no intention of marrying Maggie, but then he was struck with an awful thought. Maggie was drinking quite a lot. What if she told Peter about his, Fell's, parentage!

"So to get back to business," Melissa was saying.

The first little hair crack appeared on the lacquer of Fell's obsession. Just a little flash of irritation. Until he had seen Maggie, he had been finding Melissa's description of how she wanted to start aromatherapy treatment fascinating. He had been lost in a warm dream of her gently stroking scented oils over his body. Now he wanted her to worry with him about what on earth Maggie was talking about. The reporter couldn't fancy her, could he? Not Maggie.

Melissa was privately thinking that Maggie had set up the whole thing to make Fell jealous. It was just what she would have done herself. The little frump was positively glowing. If Fell wasn't careful, she'd be off with that reporter. Melissa suddenly smiled. And that would leave the field clear.

She had shrewdly noticed that little flash of irritation that had crossed Fell's eyes and she put a hand over his and looked deep into his eyes, and said, "Let's cut this evening short. No pudding. No coffee. You can't really listen to me properly until you get this business of Maggie and the reporter off your mind. If you don't mind me saying so, Fell, I don't think you have anything to worry about. Maggie struck me as being a bit naïve and probably thinks that reporter really fancies her."

"I'm worried about what she's telling him," said Fell.

"Forget it. You go home and deal with it and we'll meet again. I can't say I'm enjoying this evening much." Melissa signalled for the bill. Fell was immediately conscience-stricken and now consumed with the fear that he had bored her, that he was losing her.

"I am so sorry," he babbled. "Look, I am really keen to invest in your business. Can we meet soon?"

"Let's leave it a week," said Melissa briskly, thinking, let him stew for a bit.

Maggie watched them go. Fell walked past her table after Melissa without stopping to speak.

Outside the restaurant, Fell said, "Please let me see you home."

"Another time. It's a fine night." Melissa strode off. He stood with his hands hanging at his side, watching her go. Maggie's laugh rang out through the open window.

Fell was consumed with fury. Maggie would have to go. She had ruined his evening.

He walked quickly home and sat in the living room, waiting and waiting.

At last, about midnight, he heard their voices outside. What had they been doing? The restaurant closed at eleven.

The front door opened and Maggie came in. She looked

radiant because Peter had kissed her when they had been strolling along the river after dinner, and she had enjoyed it because she had imagined he was Fell.

"Just what the hell do you think you have been doing?" shouted Fell.

"I was out on a date, just like you," said Maggie defensively.

"What did you tell him, you bitch? Did you tell him I was a bastard?"

"Of course not! He likes me. He thinks I'm pretty."

"You!" said Fell with contempt.

"I'll go and pack," said Maggie quietly.

"Do that!"

Maggie was beyond tears. Slowly she went up to her room. She packed a suitcase and lugged it downstairs. "I'll come tomorrow for the rest of my stuff," she said.

Fell was sitting on the sofa with his head in his hands. He did not look up.

When Fell awoke the next morning, the memory of what had happened the night before came rushing into his head. He turned his face into the pillow. He had not had much to drink, and yet he felt he must have been drunk. He remembered Maggie saying that Peter thought her pretty and heard again his own contemptuous voice saying, "You!"

He would need to apologize to her.

He washed and dressed and went downstairs. It didn't look like a home any more. There was no Maggie making coffee in the kitchen. He walked from room to room. The sitting room stood empty, all the furniture and knick-knacks having been transported to Aunt Agnes in Wales. He walked back into the living room. It was wrong. The white walls looked stark and the new three-piece suite—well—suburban. The kitchen looked warm and inviting, but then, most of that refurbishment had been Maggie's idea. He knew the living-room furnishings were wrong, but could not think what he could do to change them. Perhaps his taste was locked for life into the working class. Melissa would know what to do.

He looked at the clock. He had slept late. It was nine-thirty. He would phone Melissa at the shop and ask her to come round and give him her advice. Eager to hear the sound of her voice, he dialled the shop number. But Melissa, who had decided that the idea of giving him time to himself was the best idea, said she was too busy. "Ask Maggie," she suggested.

"Maggie's left," said Fell heavily.

"Oh, well, I'm not surprised," said Melissa cheerfully, now feeling very sure of him. "Tell you what, I'll ring you next week. Oh, got to go. Got a customer. Byee!"

Fell slowly replaced the receiver. He felt abandoned. He could not put it off any longer. He would need to apologize to Maggie or his conscience would not give him a quiet moment.

He first had to go to the hotel to find her home address. Then he walked through the airless day, hoping he would find Maggie alone and that he would not have to meet her mother.

Maggie's home lay in a terrace of houses much like his own, but obviously containing younger people, judging from the children playing in the street. He hesitated outside the house and then went up and rang the bell. Children screamed, a car roared down the street behind him blasting heavy metal out of every open window, and an enormously fat woman looked at him over the hedge which separated Maggie's home from the neighbour's on the left.

"There doesn't seem to be anyone at home," said Fell.

"She's out looking for work."

"Mrs. Partlett?"

"No, Maggie."

"Where did she go?"

"Saw her this morning. Said she wanted work, told her to try Katy's Kitchen, that caff down Garret Lane."

"Thanks." Fell walked off down the hot street. She had only left last night. How had she managed to get a job so quickly?

Garret Lane was off the High Street. He headed in that direction. The reason why Maggie had managed to find a job so quickly was answered as he approached the café. A woman was taking down a notice from the window which said "Waitress Wanted."

The only customers in the café were a couple seated at a window table. Maggie emerged from the nether regions carrying a tray with coffee cups. The tray trembled in her hand when she saw Fell. With a sharp pang of guilt he noticed that her eyes behind her thick glasses were red with weeping. Maggie served the customers and then approached him. "I'll be round later for the rest of my things," she said. "Oh, and I forgot to give you this." She fished in the pocket of her white apron and drew out the engagement ring. Fell flushed miserably. "I always meant for you to keep it, Maggie."

"I don't want it," said Maggie.

Fell took the ring. "Look, Maggie, I'm . . ."

The door opened and a family of four walked in. "Excuse me," said Maggie. Fell stood there, irresolute. Then he decided he had best wait at home until she came round for her things and apologize then.

The day stretched before him, hot, flat and empty. Without

Maggie, he felt he had no energy to do anything. But at least when he got the painful apology over with, he would be free, free to court Melissa. Suddenly the Melissa dream came back and wrapped him round in rosy colours. With a half-smile on his lips, he walked home, unlocked the door and walked in . . .

To chaos.

Everything was topsy-turvy. Drawers hung out at crazy angles, papers were strewn across the floor.

He felt as if he had been punched in the stomach. He walked into the kitchen, picking his way over the kitchen utensils which had been thrown over the floor out of upended drawers. How had they got in? The front door had been locked and the panes of glass on the back door and windows were intact.

He would have to phone the police. But instead he picked up the phone book and searched it until he found the phone number of Katy's Kitchen and dialled it. Maggie answered the phone.

"Maggie," gasped Fell. "We've been broken into. They seem to have gone through everything."

"Have you phoned the police?"

"No, I just got here."

"Phone them. I'll be round."

Fell phoned the police. No, he didn't know if anything of value had been taken. He had just got back. They said they would be round and he sat down on the sofa, noticing as he did so that the upholstery had been slashed.

In a short time, two policemen arrived. Fell's frightened thoughts flew to the cash box still buried in the garden. He had not checked with the lawyer or the bank as to whether the money from his inheritance had been paid into his account. He had planned to pay for the dinner the night before, although, as it had turned out, Melissa had paid. But the day before, he had dug up the cash box and taken money out of it before replacing it and filling in the hole. He had made a hurried job of it. What if the police dug it up?

He gathered his wits and followed them from room to room. The few things of value, such as the television, were still there. Maggie arrived and exclaimed at the chaos. They both made statements and were warned not to touch anything until the place had been examined for fingerprints.

"How did they get in?" asked Maggie.

"There's no sign of a break-in," said Fell.

"You've only got a Yale lock on your front door," said one of the policemen. Maggie suddenly remembered that she had never got in touch with a security firm after Andy's visit. "Easy to open with a credit card. Better get yourself a decent lock. You're lucky. The forensic team should be here any moment. It's a quiet day."

Sure enough, just as he had finished, the men in white overalls arrived. "I hope all this hasn't made you lose your job," said Fell to Maggie. Her eyes were still red and his heart ached for her.

"As a matter of fact, it has," said Maggie with a shrug. "But I'll get another one soon enough. There's a shortage of waitresses."

"You could always . . . ," began Fell, but just then, the doorbell rang.

Fell opened the door. A large crumpled man stood on the doorstep. He was carrying his jacket over his arm. His wrinkled shirt was stretched over his stomach. His voluminous trousers sagged down to his dusty shoes. His face, like his clothes, looked sagging and crumpled. There were great pouches under his eyes. His thick greyish lips were permanently turned down at the corners, and small intelligent eyes stared at Fell from under fleshy lids.

"Detective Inspector Dunwiddy," he said.

"Fell Dolphin. Come in."

"You've had a burglary?"

"It looks more of a search."

Dunwiddy followed him into the living room and stood looking around, dwarfing the small room with his bulk. "Better not disturb the fingerprint work," he said. "Got a garden at the back?"

"Yes."

"We'll take chairs out there. Is this Maggie Partlett?"

"Yes, how did you . . . ?"

"Read about you pair in the local paper."

Fell and Maggie collected chairs from the kitchen and then exchanged nervous glances as they carried them out into the back garden, for the plot where the cash box was buried looked glaringly obvious to them.

"Lucky this bit's in the shade," said Dunwiddy, sitting down with a sigh. "Now, the situation is this: There's been a lot of break-ins recently, all for drugs. Telly, videos, stereos, jewellery taken to hawk for drugs. But you say nothing's really been taken, and that's what interests me. It appears in the paper that you are researching that old train robbery, and hey, presto, someone or some people break in and ransack the place. So it looks to me as if someone's worried you've found something, or someone thinks your father might have hidden cash from that robbery."

"My father was innocent," said Fell defiantly.

"Maybe. Anyway, you've got someone rattled and that's the

way I see it. Phoned your lawyer before I came here. Rumour in this town is that you've been left a good bit of money. Lawyer says your parents were right misers and never spent a penny. Right?"

"Right," echoed Fell.

"So if you've got someone worried, then to me that means that someone who had a hand in the robbery is still around. Well, you amateur detectives, how far have you got?"

"Not very far," said Fell. "Have we, Maggie?"

Maggie took off her glasses and passed a hand wearily over her eyes. "No," she said. "We got a book on the robbery out of the library and we spoke to the other signalman, Terry Weal, and then the editor of the paper. Oh, and Inspector Rudfern."

"You wouldn't get far with him," snorted Dunwiddy. "Arrogant bastard. He thinks because he couldn't solve it, nobody can. Then we come to a chap called Andy Briggs."

Fell wanted to look at Maggie but was aware that the big detective was studying them carefully.

"Wasn't that the name of the fellow who was murdered recently?" he said as casually as he could.

"The same. Now he was Tarry Briggs's boy, and Tarry Briggs was our only sure suspect. Did a runner to Spain and lived like a king. The point is this: What did Andy Briggs come back for?"

The gun, thought Maggie with a stab of panic. They'll find the gun!

Fell had the same thought at the same moment. Should they say anything or sit it out and pray that the forensic team wouldn't look in that suitcase under the bed where Maggie had hidden it?

Suddenly overcome with fright and distress, Maggie began to cry.

"There, now, miss." Dunwiddy stood up and put a heavy hand on her shoulder. "When they're finished here, try to get a rest before you clean up. I'll call back tomorrow and we'll take it from there. Don't worry; I'll see myself out."

Fell waited until he heard the street door slam, then he handed Maggie a clean handkerchief. She blew her nose and said in a shaky voice, "The gun. What if they find the gun?"

"We'll wait and see," whispered Fell. He took her hand in his. "I'm sorry about last night, Maggie. You *are* pretty. Honest. I was just mad at you. Frightened you might have let something slip to that reporter about my birth. I'm sorry."

"It's all right," said Maggie wearily. "I don't think anything matters much any more."

They sat side by side in silence.

At last Fell said, "I think I hear them packing up. I'll go and look. If they'd found that gun, Maggie, the detective would have been back here like a shot or a least one of them would have brought it out and asked you where you had got it."

"I've thought of something else," said Maggie, turning a muddy colour.

"What? What is it?"

"I didn't wipe the gun. It'll have my fingerprints on it, yours, and Andy Briggs's."

"I'm sure they're leaving," said Fell. "Wait here."

So Maggie waited, hugging herself, feeling cold despite the heat of the day.

She could hear the murmur of voices and then the street door slammed. Fell came back. "They've gone. Let's go and look."

Together they went indoors and up the stairs, Maggie leading the way to her old room. The suitcase, the one she had not taken with her, was poking out from under the bed, covered in fingerprint dust. She pulled it out and threw back the lid. She searched frantically among the clothes. She turned a white face up to him. "It's not here!"

"Then they didn't find it," said Fell grimly. "Whoever searched the house did."

Maggie raised a shaking hand to her mouth. "I'm frightened."

Fell took her hands and raised her to her feet. "You're going to have to move back in, Maggie."

"Why?"

"Because we're going to have to look out for each other from now on, and we can't do that from opposite ends of the town."

"But Melissa . . ."

"I'll continue to see Melissa, but I think we should stick together."

Maggie wavered. "I couldn't stand another quarrel, Fell."

"Then we'll just need to make sure we don't have another. Let's go downstairs and have a stiff drink."

Maggie followed him down, her thoughts in a jumble. She felt she should be glad that the quarrel was over, but all she felt was a shaky mixture of fright and weariness.

Fell poured two stiff whiskies and handed one to Maggie. "This furniture is ruined," he said.

"I think an upholsterer could repair it."

"I don't think I want it repaired. It's wrong, suburban, but I don't know what it should look like."

"I didn't like to say anything at the time," ventured Maggie. "But I do have a suggestion."

"What?"

"There's a second-hand furniture shop just out of town. They have some pretty pieces, not matching, but good stuff. You could trade this lot for part of the price. They could repair this and get a good price for it."

"What sort of things?"

"Well, there's some pretty fruitwood furniture. Some of it's Dutch. We could have a look after we've cleared this up. Perhaps if we work all day on it, we'll feel tired, but not so worried."

"You're a good sort, Maggie," said Fell. Melissa had retreated to a corner of his mind. He would not admit it to himself for fear of losing his dream, but he had been annoyed at Melissa's dismissal of him when he had needed her help.

"Let's finish our drinks and get started."

"Why don't you go and bring back your stuff and we can settle everything first?"

"Right." Maggie drained her drink and then said shyly, "And it's all right if I go on seeing Peter?"

"Yes," said Fell, although he did not like the idea one bit. The doorbell rang and they both jumped.

"What now?" asked Fell, going to answer it.

His face darkened when he found Peter and a photographer standing on the doorstep.

"Little bird told me you had been burgled," said Peter.

"You'd better come in," said Fell coldly.

Peter breezed past him, followed by his photographer. He stooped and gave Maggie a smacking kiss on the cheek. Fell was at first glad in a mean little part of his soul that Maggie was looking such a mess, but Peter sat down beside her and took her hand. "Oh, will there have to be a story on this?" wailed Maggie.

"Do you some good, love," said Peter. "Let the buggers know you've got the press on your side. Now go and put some make-up on that pretty face and pose for a nice picture."

"My make-up isn't here. It's at home," said Maggie.

"What's it doing at home? Home, home? I mean, I thought this was your home."

"It is," said Maggie. "But I was sorting things out."

"I'll get you something. Be back in a tick."

Fell waited, irritated, while Maggie made coffee for the photographer in the kitchen by dint of scooping some instant coffee into a cup from the pile of it on the kitchen counter. The searcher, or searchers, had even tipped out the contents of the coffee jar.

When Peter returned, he said cheerfully, "Let's go up to your bathroom and I'll make you up. Did I ever tell you I used to be in amateur theatricals?"

Fell made desultory conversation with the photographer while listening to Maggie's laugh floating down the stairs. What right had Maggie to be so cheerful in the middle of all this mess?

When they finally came down the stairs, Fell said sharply, "What have you done to her? She looks like a clown."

"Trust me," said Peter. "She'll look great in the photograph."

So Maggie and Fell posed amongst the ruins while the photographer snapped away busily. "Now," said Peter, "that bit's over. What happened?"

Fell described how he had gone out and when he had come back it was to find the chaos.

"So someone must have been watching the house," said Peter. "What did they take?"

"Nothing," said Maggie quickly.

"Aha. So whoever it was must be connected to that train robbery."

"What makes you say that?" asked Maggie faintly.

"Stands to reason. A story appears about you two in the newspaper, about how you're trying to find out the truth about the train robbery. Someone gets nervous and wonders if you've found out anything."

"Couldn't it just have been an ordinary burglary?" asked Maggie.

Peter snorted. "What? When they've even ripped up the upholstery?"

"Is that all?" said Fell wearily.

But Peter asked more questions: How had they felt when they saw the mess; what do they think would have happened if they had come back and surprised the burglar? Maggie shuddered, remembering that gun.

"It was someone experienced," Fell said. "There was no sign of a break-in."

"So you're going on with your investigations?"

"This has made me even more determined," said Fell, although he did not feel determined at all.

Finally Peter left, whispering to Maggie as he went, "Phone me."

"Well," said Maggie faintly. "Let's get started."

†

They worked diligently for the rest of the day, tidying and cleaning. "We'll go to that second-hand furniture place you were talking about," said Fell. "We'll go in the morning."

Tired though Maggie was, a little glow of happiness was beginning to spread inside her. She and Fell were working together again.

They both slept late the next morning. Once he was dressed, Fell said he would go out and get a copy of the *Buss Courier*. He was just emerging from the newspaper shop when he bumped into his lawyer. "How are things going, Mr. Dolphin?" asked Mr. Jamieson.

"Not very well. I had a burglary yesterday."

"Yes, I heard about that," said Mr. Jamieson. "I believe it's in the paper."

"I'm thinking of going into business," said Fell. "I meant to call round and ask you how soon my inheritance will be in the bank."

"It's all wound up. The cheque should be in your bank by now. What kind of business were you thinking of going into?"

"That health shop in the High Street."

"Wait until I get my paper. I would like to talk to you about that."

Fell looked at the newspaper while he waited for the lawyer. He and Maggie were photographed on the front page. Maggie did not look at all like Maggie. She looked quite beautiful. "Threat to Our Detectives," said the headline.

The lawyer emerged. "Let's go to my office for a chat."

"I really should be getting back to Maggie."

"You can phone her from my office."

They walked together to the lawyer's office in the town

square. The market was in full swing. On such a day, thought Fell, did I learn of my inheritance.

Once in the office, he phoned Maggie and said he was at the lawyer's and would be back shortly.

"Sit down, Mr. Dolphin," said Mr. Jamieson. "I assume you are talking about going into business with Mrs. Melissa Harley."

"Yes."

"You must realize, Mr. Dolphin," said the lawyer, "that this is a small market town and gossip spreads quickly, particularly in the Rotary club, of which I am a member. Mrs. Harley is running into financial difficulties. The business rates in this town are quite high and her shop is in a prime site in the High Street. I believe it was suggested to her that she choose a more modest place to start her business, but she would not listen. The majority of people in this town like smoking and junk food. She has only a short lease on the shop, so she would not get all that much for it if she sold now. Mrs. Harley almost got a businessman to invest in her shop, but, if you understand me, his wife stepped in and stopped it. I feel it is my duty to advise you that you would be throwing your inheritance away."

Fell turned red. "I don't believe you," he said passionately.

"You do not need to. All you have to do is bring her to me and ask her to bring her books with her. If she has nothing to worry about, she will do so."

"Thank you," said Fell coldly. "Will that be all?"

"Yes, but do be cautious."

I hate this nasty little town, thought Fell furiously as he walked through the market. It's a hotbed of false and malicious gossip.

He met the editor of the *Buss Courier,* Tommy Whittaker. "If it isn't Mr. Dolphin," said the editor cheerfully. "Good story, hey?"

Fell looked blankly down at his hand as if expecting to see the newspaper still there. "I haven't read it," he said. "I must have left it somewhere." He looked at the editor and suddenly burst out with, "Do you know Melissa Harley?"

"Oh, Harpy Harley, the one that runs the health shop? Why?"

"Nothing."

"So why ask?" Tommy's red-veined eyes sharpened. "Got nothing to do with the robbery, has she?"

"Of course not," snapped Fell. He brushed past the editor and walked rapidly away.

But instead of going home, he went round to the High Street and positioned himself opposite Melissa's shop. He watched.

He watched for an hour. No one went in and no one came out.

SIX

†

MAGGIE looked up as Fell came in. His face looked grey. "What's the matter?" she asked sharply. "No inheritance?"

"It's just the heat," said Fell. "Leave me alone." He sank down on the ruined sofa and stared bleakly ahead.

Maggie went into the kitchen. She made a cup of coffee and tipped a measure of whisky into it. She took it in and handed it to Fell. "Drink that," she ordered. "It's good for shock."

"I haven't had a shock," protested Fell.

But he drank the coffee while Maggie watched him. "Was it something in the newspaper?" asked Maggie. "I was worried about you. You were away for ages."

Fell pulled a crumpled copy of the newspaper from his pocket. He had bought another one. Maggie smoothed it out. "Oh, I do look good," she exclaimed. "Doesn't look like me at all." She read quickly. "It's just a straightforward account. So it can't be that. It's something you don't want to talk about, isn't it, Fell?"

He nodded.

"Then we won't talk about it," said Maggie briskly. "Action is the best thing. If you've finished your coffee, we'll go to that furniture place. And we'd better get a locksmith to put a lock on the door and perhaps a burglar alarm. I'll look up the business directory, shall I?"

Fell nodded dumbly.

He sat, aware of Maggie's voice on the phone, but lost in thoughts about Melissa. He should have known she was after his money. Maggie replaced the receiver. "A man from a security firm out on the estate will be round at four this afternoon. Come on, dear, let's get moving."

Fell followed her out. How odd that it should be so sunny. It ought to be black and cold and raining. Somehow the sunshine intensified pain. He got into Maggie's little car feeling stiff and old, as if the hurt had invaded his bones like a kind of emotional rheumatism.

Melissa, thought Maggie bitterly. I could kill her!

She said nothing, but drove to the second-hand furniture shop. "You choose what you think we ought to have," said Fell.

"If you're sure. You're the one that's going to be living with it."

"I'm sure." Fell offered a lame excuse. "It's just the heat, Maggie, and delayed shock about finding out about my real parents."

Maggie hesitated. "Before I choose anything, Fell, you once said you would like to turn the living room into a large kitchen and use the sitting room as a living room. It would cost a bit, but you could get the wall between the kitchen and the living room knocked down and make it all into one big kitchen."

Fell remembered his dream of a warm country kitchen. "Good idea. But you're right. We'll start using the sitting room."

They went into the huge shop together. Despite his misery, Fell was surprised at the quality of the furniture. Some of it was antique and very expensive indeed. "I'll just sit here," said Fell, taking a chair at the door. "Get what you think is best."

Maggie hesitated a moment and then went off. After an hour, she had chosen a comfortable leather armchair for Fell, a large down-stuffed sofa, an easy chair with a wide Victorian seat upholstered in green velvet, two occasional chairs, a writing table, and a coffee table. She told Fell the price. The assistant said they would send someone round this afternoon to give them a price on their ruined furniture, and if everything was agreeable they would deliver the new furniture the following day. Maggie told him to send their man round at four, judging she could deal with the security firm and the furniture people in one go.

When she then told Fell what she had done, he said, "Fine."

She then suggested they go somewhere for a snack. She drove them to a pub. Fell ate an omelette and drank half a pint of beer in silence. Maggie was becoming increasingly worried about him.

When they went back home, Fell said, "Do you mind if I go up to bed?"

"No, you go ahead," said Maggie. "I'll handle everything."

"I'll sign some blank cheques," said Fell. "Just fill in what they need."

The locksmith arrived and fitted a new Yale lock, and a mortise, and two bolts. He then, on Maggie's instructions, fitted bolts at the top and bottom of the kitchen door. Maggie paid him from Fell's cheque book. He had left three signed cheques for her.

Then the furniture man arrived and tut-tutted at the ripped upholstery but offered Maggie a figure which was better than she expected. That was deducted from the price of the newly bought furniture. Two men carried the three-piece suite out. Maggie handed over a cheque, and the new furniture was carried into the sitting room.

Then the burglar alarm system was installed, and Maggie carefully listened to the instructions. The police, said the man, would turn out twice a year for false alarms, but any more and they would not come at all.

When they had all finished, Maggie went into the sitting room. She was pleased with the furniture. She took two lamps they had brought through from the living room and plugged them in. Then she took down the William Morris–patterned curtains from the living room and replaced the nasty, dusty velvet ones in the sitting room with them. They had replaced the fitted carpet in the living room with colourful rugs. She carried some of them into the sitting room and spread them on the floor. She surveyed her work with satisfaction. The odd mixture of furniture worked very well.

Maggie then went quietly up the stairs and looked into Fell's room. He was lying asleep on top of the bed.

She decided to leave him to sleep. She drove home and collected the suitcase she had packed the night before and then took down two paintings from the walls of her room. She had picked both up at an auction. One was a seascape and the other was a bucolic countryside scene.

When she got back to Fell's, she hung the pictures in the

sitting room, switched on the lamps, and then went in and arranged a bottle of whisky, glasses, a jug of water and some crisps and nuts in bowls and carried them into the sitting room, just as she heard Fell come down the stairs.

He came into the sitting room, rubbing his eyes. "Sorry I've slept so long. Oh, this is *nice,* Maggie."

He sank down on the new sofa. "Goodness, pictures, too."

Maggie wanted to ask him if he felt like talking, but bit back the question as it rose to her lips. It would be something to do with Melissa and she did not want to hear anything about Melissa, good or bad, ever again.

The phone rang and Fell jumped. "I'll get it," said Maggie. "We'd better get an extension cord tomorrow and move the phone in here."

Maggie went into the living room and picked up the receiver. It was Peter. "Can you talk?" he asked.

"Yes."

"What about coming out for a drink?"

"Not tonight."

"Tomorrow?"

"Yes, all right. Where?"

"The Red Lion, say about nine. I finish work then."

"Okay."

Maggie replaced the receiver and went back to Fell.

"Who was it?" he asked.

"Just Peter. I'm meeting him for a drink tomorrow night. Is that all right?"

"Of course it is. Does he know we're not really engaged?"

"No, I haven't told him."

"Might be a good idea not to tell him yet, Maggie."

"Why?"

"You don't really know him. Might be safer to hold back from telling him until you do." He fished in his pocket and brought out the engagement ring. "You may as well put this back on, Maggie. People will wonder why you're not wearing it."

Maggie longed to ask him to put it on her finger so that she could pretend for a moment that she really was engaged, but quietly took it from him and slipped it on her finger instead.

Maggie said, "I've got the new door keys. We've a set each. You'd better come through and I'll show you how the burglar alarm works."

They were standing at the front door, examining the control box, when the doorbell rang.

Maggie opened the door. It was Detective Inspector Dunwiddy. "Just thought I'd drop by for another chat."

"Come in. We've just had a burglar alarm installed," said Maggie, chattering brightly because the sight of the inspector unnerved her. "We've moved to the sitting room."

The inspector followed them to the sitting room. "Nice," he said, looking round and unconsciously echoing Fell.

"Sit down," said Maggie effusively. "Whisky?"

"Don't mind if I do. Not too strong and lots of water."

The inspector settled back in his chair, cradling his glass in his large hands. "So," he said, "this break-in interests me. I'm off duty but I thought I'd have a chat with you. I see you've cleared up. Find anything of value missing?"

"No," said Fell.

Dunwiddy looked at Maggie's hands. "I see you've got an expensive ring there. You weren't wearing it when I last called. You're lucky they didn't take it."

"I take it off for work. I was working in Katy's Kitchen when Fell called about the burglary."

"Well, it looks definitely like whoever it was thought you might have found out something. Or it could be someone thought your father was involved in the train robbery and had hidden the money somewhere. That would explain why even jars of coffee and flour had been tipped out."

"But the thief would surely be someone who was involved in the robbery and who would therefore know my father had no part in it."

"We've never really been sure about that. Or it could be someone who'd heard you'd come into money and was looking for some of it. I think there must have been more than one. Someone to watch and report when you left, someone to warn the thief when you were coming back."

He drank a great gulp of whisky. "It's all very odd after all those years. Such a coincidence Andy Briggs coming back. Hadn't a penny and signed on for the dole. There was something odd came up at the autopsy as well."

Fell and Maggie stared at him like rabbits caught in a headlights' glare. "Oh, he died of knife wounds, that's for sure. But he'd a great bump on his head. Just before he died, someone had hit him very hard over the head with something heavy."

"Maybe it happened during the fight," suggested Maggie, amazed that her own voice sounded quite calm.

"No. Too many witnesses to the fight. Mind you, he seemed to have a way of getting folks riled up, particularly when he was drunk. Took after his old man. Did your father ever say anything about Tarry Briggs?"

"I can't remember anything at the moment," said Fell. "He

sometimes would talk to my mother about passengers. He was very impressed by what he called the nobs. But I never heard him discuss the railway workers."

The inspector drained his glass. He stood up. "Go carefully now. And if you remember anything or notice anything strange, let me know."

Fell saw him to the door. "Did you question the neighbours?" he asked nervously. "I mean, did any of them notice anyone in the street outside who might be suspicious?"

"No one but the postman delivering a parcel."

"But there was no parcel," said Fell excitedly. "It must have been someone masquerading as the postman. The post comes very early, about seven in the morning."

"Ah, well, now, that's interesting. We'd better check the theatrical costumer's down in the Foregate and ask at the main post office whether anyone's missing a uniform."

After Dunwiddy had left, Fell returned to Maggie and told her about the postman.

"Do you know," said Maggie, "I don't think anyone would need to go to the lengths of renting a costume to look like a postman. Any sort of peaked cap would do. And a blue shirt or sweater. The badge could be faked up from any of those plastic badges with funny slogans on them."

"That's true," said Fell.

"You must be hungry." Maggie headed for the kitchen, calling over her shoulder. "I'll make us something to eat."

"No. Wait!"

Maggie went back into the sitting room. "I feel like getting out of here."

"Where?"

"Anywhere."

"It's a bit late, but there's that place on the motorway we went to before."

"That'll do."

"Right. Let's see if we can set the burglar alarm."

Half an hour later, they were sitting eating chicken and chips. "I remember," said Fell, "when chicken used to taste quite different. We always had chicken for Christmas when I was very small. Roast chicken. And it had such a flavour."

"It's all the junk and hormones they put in things these days. It's not very nice, is it? But it's great to get out. And there's air-conditioning here."

"I keep wondering if we should get air-conditioning," said Fell.

"Waste of money. We won't see another summer like this for a long time." Maggie sighed. "Dandelion summer. Are you feeling better, by the way?"

"Why do you ask?"

"When you came back this morning, you looked shattered."

"Oh, it's just because all this is getting on top of me," lied Fell. He found he could not conjure up a picture of Melissa. He was so badly hurt that his mind shrank away from any image of her.

"So do we go on?" asked Maggie.

"With the investigation? Yes, I think we should." Anything to keep his mind off health shops and Melissa, thought Fell.

"Where should we start?"

"Johnny Tremp, I think. We'll try that address in the phone book tomorrow."

†

As they set out the following morning, the news reader on Maggie's car radio was warning of water shortages. There was a hosepipe ban. There had been more fires on the Malvern Hills. In the village of Broadway in Gloucestershire, a famous beauty spot, the river had sunk to an all-time low. Meanwhile Scotland was suffering from flash floods and torrential rain. "Isn't it amazing," said Maggie, "that such a small country as Britain should have such diverse climates? I wish they'd send some of their water down here."

"Turn left here," said Fell, who was studying a street map. "Let me see. Right. That's it. Go slowly. Yes, that's the place right here."

It was a rundown-looking council house among other depressing-looking houses. In most of the housing estates in Buss, the residents had bought their houses, put into new windows, painted the outside, planted pretty gardens, but here, there was a sad feeling of neglect all around.

Fell and Maggie walked up to a chipped and scarred door. Fell knocked. After a few moments, the door was opened by a tired-looking girl. She was holding a baby on her hip and two toddlers were hanging on to her skirts. Her black hair was cropped close to her head and her figure looked too thin and emaciated to have borne three children.

"We're looking for Mr. Tremp," he said.

"He don't live here no more, not for a couple of years."

"This address is still in the phone book."

"I ain't got a phone and that's his business."

"So do you know where I can find him?" asked Fell patiently.

"Heard he'd gone to some village over in Gloucestershire. Funny name. Somethink about hedges."

"Had he any friends in this street, any family who might know where he's gone?"

From the interior of the house, the opening music of a soap could be heard.

"Gotta go," she said quickly and slammed the door on them.

"So what do we do now?" asked Maggie as they walked to the car.

"Try next door."

This time it was a surly man smelling of stale beer. Fell explained they were looking for Johnny Tremp. "Blessed if I know," said the man. "He kept hisself to hisself, know what I mean?"

"We heard he'd gone to some village, something like Hedges."

"That'd be Bramley-in-the-Hedges, t'other side o' Moreton." His eyes sharpened. "You the social?" he asked truculently. "Well, let me tell you, I never laid a hand on those kids."

"No, we're not from the social security."

"So who are you?"

Fell explained about the robbery.

"Oh, you're that pair. Saw a bit about you in the *Courier*. Hey, you think grumpy Tremp was in on that?"

"No, no," said Fell quickly. "Still just asking questions."

"Doubt if he had anything to do with it, mate. Had a dirty old car on its last legs. Never did anything to the house."

"Thanks," said Fell, taking Maggie's hand and backing away. Maggie could feel something like an electric shock running up her arm and was relieved when Fell released her hand at the garden gate.

"Do you know where this Bramley-in-the-Hedges is?" asked Maggie, once they were in the car.

"Wait; I've got the road map here." Fell always had lots of maps. He loved maps. He used to pore over them when his parents were alive: all those roads leading away from Buss.

"I've found it," he said. "Go to Moreton-in-Marsh and make a right after the bridge and I'll direct you from there."

Bramley-in-the Hedges turned out to be one of those long villages mainly consisting of one main street, full of winding bends to enrage the motorist. Maggie suggested they stop at the village's general store in the centre and ask for directions. The shop, like all converted village shops, was a sort of tiny supermarket. There were several people chatting and shopping.

They went up to the counter. "Can I help you?" asked the woman behind the counter. She was round and plump with a friendly, cheerful face. Maggie smiled. "Can you direct us to where Mr. Johnny Tremp lives?"

The woman's eyes hardened. Behind them in the shop was a sudden silence.

"Are you friends of his?"

"Not exactly," began Fell. "You see . . ."

"Then don't come in here asking for people's private address. If you don't want to buy anything, get along with you."

They made their way out, aware of hostile stares from the shoppers. Outside, Fell ran his long fingers through his thick grey hair in bewilderment. "What was all that about?"

"I don't know," said Maggie. "We'll take a look around. It seems a pretty small village. Can you remember what he looks like?"

"It was years ago. He was a small man with black hair. Oh, I remember, he had very thick lips. They used to fascinate and repel me."

"Not much to go on. But let's try to find him anyway."

"There's a phone box," said Fell. "We could try to get his number from directory enquiries."

"Good idea."

It was one of those old-fashioned red telephone boxes, hot and stifling on the inside. Fell dialled 192 and asked for the phone number of a Mr. J. Tremp, Bramley-in-the-Hedges.

"That number is ex-directory," said the operator.

For the next hour, they walked up one side of the main street and down the other and then up several lanes which wound off from the main street on either side.

"I'm so tired and hot and sticky," mourned Maggie.

"I wonder," said Fell. "I just wonder."

"What?"

"We've been assuming he would live in a modest house. But what if he was in on the train robbery and sat on the money for years? He would buy somewhere big."

"I can't see any big houses."

"There are usually some just outside a village like this."

"Then we'll take the car," said Maggie. "I can't walk any more."

They walked back to Maggie's car and drove out of the village. "There's a couple of gate posts," said Fell. "Drive in there, Maggie."

"This would be too grand, surely," said Maggie.

"But someone grand might not be as close-mouthed as the people in the village," said Fell. "In fact, the farther we get away from the village, the better chance we have of someone talking. There seems to be a sort of conspiracy of silence in the village itself."

"This *is* grand," said Maggie as a large Cotswold manor house came into view. "And we're trespassing."

"We've come this far," said Fell. "You stay in the car if you like."

Maggie nodded.

She saw Fell go up to the main door, which stood open. A man came round the corner of the house and shouted to Fell, "What do you want?"

Fell went up to him. Maggie's heart lifted as she saw the man begin to answer Fell's question and then point to the west.

Fell came back. "I've got it," he said excitedly. "Johnny Tremp lives in a large bungalow on the other side of the village. It's called Beechwood."

"Great," said Maggie. "Although I am so tired and hot and hungry, I'll be glad when we finally see him and then we can get a cold drink and some late lunch."

As they drove back through the village, some people were standing outside the village stores. They turned and stared at the car as it went past.

Maggie giggled. "It's like one of those American small-town horror movies. All we need now is the corrupt sheriff."

"Maybe it's like the Stepford Wives and they've all been taken over by aliens," said Fell and began to laugh. Maggie laughed as well, delighted that Fell seemed to have risen out from whatever gloom had plagued him.

On the other side of the road, Maggie drove slowly until they saw a large new bungalow up on a rise. It was surrounded by a high fence. Two large steel gates at the entrance to a short drive stood open, but Fell noticed with surprise that the gates were electronically operated. He pointed this fact out to Maggie and said, "We're lucky they're open."

"Should we park outside?" asked Maggie nervously. "And walk up?"

"No, just drive in. I say, Maggie, it's a big, very new building. Surely it must have taken a lot of money, and for those fences and electronic gates."

The car windows were open and Maggie could hear dogs barking. "I've got a bad feeling about this," she said.

"Then stay in the car."

"No, I think I should be with you on this one."

They parked and got out. The cold glass eye of a video camera over the door stared down at them.

Before they could ring the doorbell, it jerked open. The man facing them was old and squat and burly. He had very thick lips.

"Mr. Tremp?" asked Fell.

"Who's asking?"

"I'm Fell Dolphin. I believe you knew my father."

"So what?"

"I wondered if we could have a talk."

"I've got no time for you. I was expecting a delivery. Get the hell out of here or I'll set the dogs on you."

"But—"

He turned and walked back into the house. "Get to the car. Quick!" said Fell. "I think he really is going to set the dogs on us."

They jumped into the car and slammed the doors, just as two large Alsatians erupted from the house. Maggie sped off, the great dogs bounding on either side of the car. Only when they were out on the road and well clear of the house did the dogs fall back. Maggie drove on a little and then stopped the car and leaned her head on the steering wheel.

"All right?" asked Fell anxiously.

"I was frightened to death," said Maggie, raising her head. "We'll find a pub and have lunch."

"But don't you see, we're on to something at last!" said Fell excitedly. "How could he afford a set-up like that?"

"Maybe we should tell Dunwiddy."

"That inspector? I don't think so, Maggie. I didn't like the way he asked about Andy Briggs. I tell you what, we'll come after dark and watch the house and see who goes in and out."

"You forget, I've got a date."

"Oh, yes, him. Well, tomorrow."

"Maybe tomorrow, we could try to find that other one."

"You mean Fred Flint? There wasn't a number for him in the phone book."

"Maybe we can look at the voters' role in the library and find him. Or I'll ask Peter."

"No, don't," said Fell sharply. "I don't want that reporter to know anything we're doing."

They had lunch at the White Hart Royal in Moreton and then drove back to Buss.

Fell had fallen silent again. "I've got some housekeeping to do," said Maggie. "What about you?"

"I think I'll go out for a bit," said Fell.

"Where?"

"Just out," said Fell crossly.

Melissa again, thought Maggie bitterly.

Fell went upstairs and washed and changed into a clean

shirt and jeans. He could hear Maggie working in the kitchen. Ashamed of his bad temper, he called out, "I'm going to the bank before it closes. We don't want the neighbours to see us digging up the cash box any time we want money."

"Right," called Maggie.

Fell did go to the bank and drew out a substantial sum. He planned to give a good part of it to Maggie. She never asked him for money. Then he stood, irresolute, feeling the sun beating down on his head. Dreams and fantasies were essential to a man like Fell. They were what kept reality at bay. He wanted the Melissa dream back and in his heart cursed the lawyer. Surely Melissa had her pride and didn't want everyone to know that her business venture had failed. Perhaps he could advise her. Perhaps he could buy the remainder of the lease from her and start that bookshop, he thought, forgetting that the bookshop had been Maggie's idea. He had a sudden rosy dream of poetry readings in the evenings, with himself reading to a small audience and Melissa gazing on him with admiration.

He set out for the health shop. He hesitated outside the door. Melissa was sitting at the back of the shop at a desk, buffing her nails. The shop was dark and there was a soft lamp behind her. She looked quite beautiful.

He smiled and opened the door.

"Why, Fell!" she exclaimed. "How nice."

"Quiet day," said Fell, looking around.

"Oh, one gets days like this from time to time. What brings you?"

"I thought perhaps we could discuss business, go through the books together."

"You don't need to bother about fusty old ledgers. It

wouldn't mean anything to you. I mean, dear, you've not had much experience of business, have you?"

"No, but—"

"So why don't I just lock up. I know a nice café down by the river, Gerald's. We can talk there."

He knew he should protest, that he really should see those books, but he followed her weakly out of the shop, and then to her car. She drove off competently and they went to Gerald's, which was down on the riverside just below the Mayor Bridge.

Melissa found them a table in the café garden beside the river. "Let's not talk business until we have tea."

She was wearing a silky dress of peacock colours. She chatted about a film she had seen the night before as she poured tea and ate cream cakes. "Now, my little businessman," she said, throwing a flirtatious look at Fell, "are you ready to come in with me?"

Fell clasped his hands together and looked at her beseechingly. "The fact is, Melissa, that I discussed your proposition with my lawyer and he says your business is in financial difficulties."

"You didn't trust me? Really, Fell, you are no gentleman."

"If you are not in financial difficulties, then there is no problem," said Fell. "We will take your accounts round to my lawyer."

She put a hand over his clasped hands and said beseechingly. "Look, Fell, I'll come clean with you. I have had a certain amount of difficulty, but I feel I am turning the corner." Her thumb stroked his wrist. "With your investment, I could expand."

Just then the sun slid from behind the trees on the opposite side of the river and cast a merciless light on Melissa's face. He saw for the first time the wrinkles at the sides of her mouth, the pouches under her eyes, and above all, the calculating avarice in those eyes.

But he still wanted his dream back and said, "I have a proposition to put to you."

"This is so sudden!"

"Seriously." He outlined his idea of buying the lease, of the bookshop.

Melissa laughed. "My dear boy, it's obvious you've spent your life waiting table. Do you think any of the cloth-heads in this little burg are going to flock to a *bookshop?* Get real!"

Fell drew his hands away and then stood up. "I have to get back to Maggie," he said.

"Oh, your little friend. I'll drive you back."

"I'd rather walk."

Fell turned and strode away. He could hear her calling to him, but he walked on.

He walked and walked in the heat, trying to walk his misery away. He felt like a wimp, like a naïve fool. He did not get home until half past eight. Maggie called down the stairs, "Is that you, Fell?"

"Yes."

"I left some quiche and salad in the kitchen for you."

"Thanks."

Fell was sitting at the table, staring at an untouched plate of food, when Maggie came into the kitchen. He looked up. She was wearing the green chiffon dress and high heels. Her hair shone and her green eyes looked large and luminous behind the new contact lenses.

Fell tried to smile. "You look much too good to be going out with Peter," he said.

"I shouldn't be too late. You look awful. What have you been up to?"

"Just walking. Walking too long in the heat. Don't worry about me."

She hesitated and then she said, "I'm off, then."

"Have fun."

Maggie went reluctantly.

Fell had looked so shattered, she longed to stay with him. She walked through the evening streets to the Red Lion. Peter was already there and she saw from his flushed face and bright watery eyes that he had already been drinking. He rose and tried to kiss her on the lips, but Maggie quickly turned her face so that a wet kiss landed on her cheek. "What'll you have?" asked Peter.

"Just orange juice," said Maggie, hoping that her choice of a non-alcoholic drink would slow him down. But he returned with an orange juice for her and a suspiciously dark glass of whisky for himself.

Fell found he was waiting and waiting for Maggie to come home. It was nearly midnight. At last he could not bear the stuffiness and silence of the little house where the ghosts of Mr. and Mrs. Dolphin seemed to be standing over him, calling him a failure. He remembered he had forgotten to give Maggie any money. The money he had drawn was upstairs in his bedside table. He went out, setting the burglar alarm, and walked to the Red Lion, but the pub was dark and closed for the night. He could not bear to return home and thought he would go down and walk along by the river. Sometimes there was a cool breeze from the water.

He made his way across the gardens to the riverside. The black water chuckled lazily past.

He was standing by the water on a little jetty used by the pleasure boats when he received an almighty shove on his back and tumbled headlong into the water. He struggled desperately to the surface, but his struggles took him out to the middle of the river.

And Fell could not swim.

SEVEN

†

MAGGIE had a horrible evening. Peter grew progressively more drunk and maudlin, yet she had neither the experience nor the courage to leave him and go home. They ended up at a noisy cellar disco which to Maggie was like a scene from hell with the smoke-filled heat of the room and the strobe lights that hurt her eyes. And then, to her relief, Peter sank down in a chair and promptly fell asleep. Guiltily, feeling that she should at least waken him and help him home, Maggie picked up her handbag and went up the stairs from the disco and took great gulps of fresh air.

She set off in the direction of home. A group of youths shouted at her, "Where you going, love?" and strung across the street, barring her way. She slipped off her high heels and ran in the opposite direction, down towards the central bridge of the town. Only once she had reached the middle of the bridge did she stop, panting. There were no sounds of pursuit. She had saved and saved to buy her little old car to take her to and from work, for Buss, which could look like something out of a Merchant Ivory film during the day, could be a dangerous place for a woman on her own at night. Drugs had crawled into every town and village in England, with the resultant crime.

The night was once more still and quiet. Then she heard a faint sound from the river below and leaned over the bridge. In the light of a security lamp in a house by the river, she saw a head rise above the water, flailing arms, and then the head disappeared. She did not stop to think. She climbed up on the parapet of the bridge and dived in. She surfaced and swam to where she had seen that head just as, with a great gasp, Fell's white face appeared above the water. She reached him and said, "Don't struggle. It's me, Maggie. Turn on your back. No don't clutch me, or we'll both go under."

He did as he was told and Maggie pulled him towards the shore. She ploughed towards a low grass bank. "You've got to help me, Fell," she said. "I'm not strong enough to pull you out."

With Fell's last remaining strength he crawled on his hands and knees up the grass and collapsed on his face. Maggie, grateful for all those swimming classes and life-saving techniques she had learned years ago, turned him on his side and began to pump the water out of him. "I'm all right," spluttered Fell weakly. "I kept my mouth closed nearly every time I went down."

"Just lie still," ordered Maggie, sitting back on her heels. She looked around in a dazed way. How quiet it was! Not a soul about to witness the drama. Maggie did not believe in God, but she suddenly remembered a mild preacher saying, "If there is no God, how do you explain coincidence?" Why should she of all people have been at the right place at the right time? If Peter had not passed out, she would still be in the disco.

Fell sat up. "I think I can make it home."

"I left my bag up on the bridge. Wait here and I'll see if it's still there."

When Maggie walked across the grass and then up the winding path which led to the bridge, she found her legs were shaking. She began to cry, tears pouring out of her eyes and down onto her soaking dress. She found her handbag where she had left it and made her way back to Fell.

He struggled to his feet when he saw her coming. "What happened?" asked Maggie.

"Someone pushed me."

"Let's get home quickly," said Maggie. The dark night was suddenly full of menace. "We'll need to call the police."

"No," said Fell, shivering despite the warmth of the night.

"Why? Someone tried to kill you."

"I don't want that Dunwiddy probing into our lives. It could have been some malicious youth, some nutter. I mean, who would know I couldn't swim?"

"Let's hurry. I'm frightened."

Fell put an arm around Maggie's waist and they hurried homewards. As they reached the town square, Maggie could hear raucous voices quite near and the sound of breaking glass. The youth of Buss, possibly her earlier tormentors, had probably smashed a shop window.

As they reached home, two police cars raced past.

Maggie forced her trembling fingers to deal with the burglar alarm. Only once they were safely inside, with the burglar alarm set, did Maggie's trembling and shaking stop.

"Let's get out of our wet clothes," she said. "Fortunately

for us, the river's unpolluted, so we shouldn't need tetanus shots. I forgot to switch the hot water on."

"We'll put it on now and change into our dressing gowns," said Fell.

Maggie clutched his arm as he was about to go up the stairs. "Do you believe in God, Fell?"

"I've never thought much about it. Why?"

"It seems so odd that I should have been there at the right time."

"I know. You saved my life and I'll never forget it."

"Oh, don't feel beholden to me in any way," said Maggie urgently.

Fell smiled at her in a way that made her heart turn over. "Impossible. Let's get out of these wet clothes."

"My new dress is ruined and I've lost my shoes," mourned Maggie. "Mind you, I sweated so much in that wretched disco, it's probably ruined anyway."

"Which disco?"

"I'll tell you sometime."

As Maggie took off her wet clothes in her bedroom and scrubbed herself down with a towel, she decided not to tell Fell that she had endured a miserable evening with Peter. He might feel she was becoming too much a permanent part of his life. She guessed his earlier misery had been caused by disillusionment about Melissa, but was shrewd enough to guess that Melissa might be soon replaced with another dream, another fantasy woman.

Maggie put the old wool dressing gown she had worn since her schooldays on over her nightgown and carefully took out her precious contact lenses, marvelling that they had not been lost in the river, popped on her thick glasses and went downstairs and began to heat up a pan of milk on the kitchen stove.

When Fell joined her, she poured two glasses of hot milk, added a dash of brandy to each, and they carried them into the sitting room.

"It really was the most amazing coincidence," said Maggie, tucking her legs under her on the sofa. "I mean, I'd left the disco to walk home and there were these youths bothering me. I ran away in the opposite direction and when I knew they weren't following me, I stopped in the middle of the bridge."

"Why didn't Peter walk you home?"

"Oh, he got called out on a story," lied Maggie quickly.

"Someone must have been following me," said Fell. "I thought I was the only one by the river. It was all so quiet. I was standing on that wooden jetty when someone gave me a great shove. I struggled to the surface but found myself out in the middle of the river. I'm frightened, Maggie. We've got the money. Why don't we go away for a bit?"

Maggie brightened. With a fantasy as rosy as anything Fell could have concocted, she conjured up a picture of both of them lying on a tropical beach under the palms.

"On the other hand," said Fell, "there's a part of me that now knows that if I run away from this, I'll consider myself a wimp and a failure for the rest of my life."

The dream burst. "Then we go on," said Maggie quietly.

"You know, Maggie, I don't think there can be anyone quite like you."

Maggie blushed with pleasure.

"I just hope Peter is worthy of you."

Maggie's heart sank. She had a sudden vision of Peter when

she had last seem him, slumped in a chair under the strobe lights, his mouth hanging open and snoring drunkenly.

"He's just a date," she mumbled.

But Fell was not paying attention. "I drew some money out of the bank. I must give you some. You never ask for any."

"You don't need to pay me. You don't owe me anything."

"Only my life. But I did draw out the money for you before you saved me. Please take some."

Maggie thought of her dwindling savings and then nodded. "Well, just some for the housekeeping."

"And a new dress. That pretty one must be ruined."

"I'll see if the dry-cleaner's can do anything with it. Let's go to bed and then we'll try that Fred Flint tomorrow."

They went upstairs and then stood together on the landing. "Good night, then," said Fell. He had a sudden impulse to kiss Maggie, but turned instead and went into his room. What on earth would Maggie think of him?

Maggie awoke during the night. She heard Fell cry out. She leaped out of bed and went to his room. He was tossing and turning and making those inarticulate strangling cries which people make when they are actually screaming in the middle of a nightmare.

Maggie sat on the end of the bed. "Shhh," she said. "Maggie's here."

The cries ceased and his sleep became calm. She stroked his hair back from his forehead with a gentle hand. She was suddenly engulfed with such a wave of love for him that she felt frightened. How could she maintain an easy, friendly manner towards him with such overwhelming love?

She went back to bed wondering why she should be cursed

with such intense feelings. Such love was for poets, not for plain Maggie Partlett.

Every morning they awoke, Fell and Maggie hoped that the stifling weather would have broken, but the next day was as close and muggy as the one before. At least at the beginning of the heatwave there had been days with a slight refreshing breeze.

They had both slept late.

"It seems odd," said Fell as they set out for the library.

"What does?"

"All last night. Like some awful dream. In fact I had an awful nightmare during the night that men were chasing me to shoot me and then a beautiful woman came into my dream and said, 'Shhh, it's all right, Fell.' "

"What did she look like, this woman?"

"Blessed if I remember."

They walked into the library. Maggie was relieved to see that the pretty librarian was not on duty. Instead there was a middle-aged, motherly woman at the desk. They asked for the voters' roll and took it over to a desk and sat side by side and began to scan the names, street by street.

"This could take all day," mourned Maggie, "and I wish it wasn't bound so that we could take a page each."

They searched on and then decided to break for a quick lunch.

After buying sandwiches and eating them on a bench outside the library, they returned to the voters' roll.

It was approaching five o'clock and Fell was just pausing to rub his tired eyes when Maggie cried triumphantly, "Got it!"

"Where?"

"Right here. Jubilee Street. Number ten."

"I saw a Jubilee Street recently," said Fell. "I know, it was when we were walking to the railway station. It's one of those roads just before you get to the station. Shall we go now? Or leave it until tomorrow?"

"May as well get it over with. We'll take the car."

They drove in silence towards Jubilee Street, each wanting to forget abut the whole thing now, but not wishing to back down in front of the other. Despite the heat, the nights were drawing in. Maggie no longer relished the idea of being out in the streets of Buss after dark.

"Turn left here," said Fell. "This is Jubilee Street and there's number ten." Maggie stopped the car. The houses had been built for the railway workers in the last century, a row of red brick cottages. They all looked well-kept.

"But no signs of great wealth," said Fell as they got out of the car.

They knocked at the door. A woman answered it. She had her hair tied up in a scarf. Fell judged her to be about the same age as himself. She had a pleasant open face.

"We're looking for Mr. Flint."

"Dad's in the garden. What's it about?"

Fell explained, bracing himself for a tirade, for no one else had been particularly friendly. But she smiled and said, "Oh, you're that pair from the newspaper. I mean, I saw the story about you. Dad'll be delighted to see you. He kept saying to me, he said, 'I could tell that pair a thing or two.' "

They followed her through the dark little house and into a long garden at the back which was a blaze of colour. A hosepipe lay on the lawn and the flowerbeds had been recently watered. "Don't you go telling the authorities I've been watering the plants," she said. "I'm not going to sit by and see all my work ruined."

There was an abundance of roses, hollyhocks, delphiniums, pansies, and gladioli crammed into flowerbeds, and in a glass-fronted shed at the bottom of the garden they could see an old man looking out at them.

"Dad, this is Dolphin's son and his girl—you know, the couple you read about in the paper."

He was a tortoise of a man, with a scrawny neck poking out of his shirt collar. He wore rimless glasses. Despite the heat of the day, his knees were covered by a rug.

"Come in," he said. "Dottie, get a couple of chairs."

"Do you mind if we sit just outside the door and talk to you?" pleaded Fell. "The heat is awful."

"We'll sit in the garden then."

The daughter brought two kitchen chairs into the garden and then her father heaved himself to his feet by the aid of two sticks. When they were all seated, Fred Flint said, "So you're wondering about that there robbery. Well, you've come to the right place."

"You know who did it?" asked Fell eagerly.

"I do that. I know three of 'em, anyway."

"Who were they?"

"Dolphin, Johnny Tremp, and Tarry Briggs."

"You mean my father . . . ?"

"Came into money, didn't you? Where d'ye think it came from?"

"I've been through the accounts and the lawyer can bear

me out. My mother and father were misers and saved every penny. They had high-interest accounts and stocks and shares. So what gives you the idea my father was in on it?"

"He was in the signal box when he should have been having a day off, wasn't he? He was the one that stopped the train."

"But he wasn't arrested and you have no proof!"

"Stands to reason he did it."

"We know about Tarry Briggs. What about Johnny Tremp?"

"He was always an evil, nasty bastard. I never liked working with him. If ever there was a villain it was Johnny Tremp."

Fell slumped in his hard little chair, suddenly weary. "But you have no real proof."

The old man tapped the side of his nose. "I know," he said.

"So who masterminded the whole thing?"

"One of those villains from London. They promised that precious three a cut of the robbery."

"Why not you?"

" 'Cause I was always as honest as the day and they knew it."

"But weren't Johnny Tremp and Tarry Briggs at work that day?"

"That's the thing. They weren't. Tarry Briggs wasn't due on duty until later and it was Johnny's day off. Funny that, hey?"

Fell would have liked to make his escape then and there, but the old man began to reminisce about days on the railway until, after an hour, when Fell thought he couldn't bear much more of it, Fred Flint fell asleep. Fell signalled to Maggie that they should leave. Dottie was working in the kitchen.

"Your father's asleep," said Fell, "and we've got another appointment."

"I'd best go and help him to bed. You will call again, won't you? The company does him good."

Feeling guilty, Fell said they would call again although he had no intention of doing so.

"So what now?" asked Maggie.

"It's dark now. We could go to Bramley-in-the-Hedges and watch Johnny Tremp's for a little. Watch who comes and goes."

"All right," said Maggie, "but let's find a place where we can't be seen from his house. Those dogs terrify me."

They stopped a little away from Johnny Tremp's house where they could watch the gates. Maggie had parked the car under a stand of trees whose branches all but blocked a view of the house, but the little they could see was enough. There was a bright security light above the door of the bungalow which lit up the front of the house and the drive.

They had been there an hour when suddenly Maggie became aware that Fell had covered his face with his hands and was shaking. "What is it, Fell?"

"I'm falling apart," he said. "It's all come down on me, Maggie. My birth, the robbery, Andy Briggs, the attempt on my life, everything."

"We're going home," said Maggie. "It's delayed shock. Hang on. I'll soon have us back home."

Fell had lost his enthusiasm for cooking, so it was usually Maggie, armed with new cookery books, who prepared the meals. After they had eaten, she suggested that Fell go to bed. Just then the phone rang.

"If it's Melissa, tell her I'm out," said Fell quickly. "I don't feel like talking business."

Maggie picked up the phone. It was Peter.

"I'm sorry about the other night," said Peter. "Don't know what came over me, falling asleep like that. Must have been doing too much."

Doing too much drinking, thought Maggie.

"Anyway," Peter went on cheerfully, "I'm reporting on a fashion show over in Cheltenham Town Hall tomorrow afternoon. Too far off our track usually for the *Courier,* but this one's high-fashion clothes—Versace, Gucci, Armani—all those bods. Like to come? I could pick you up at two o'clock."

"I don't think so," said Maggie. "I think Fell and I are doing something. Wait a minute." She turned to Fell. "It's Peter. He wants to take me to some fashion show at Cheltenham Town Hall tomorrow."

"Then why not go?" asked Fell. "I wouldn't mind a quiet day here."

Maggie quickly masked her disappointment. "All right, Peter," she said.

"Grand," he said. "The photographer's making his own way."

"How long does the show last?"

"An hour and a half."

And then, thought Maggie, what? If he phones over his story, it will be a tour of the pubs all the way back to Buss.

"I've got something to do earlier in Cheltenham, Peter," she said. "I'll take my car and meet you there."

"I'll wait for you outside. The show starts at three."

"See you." Maggie put down the receiver.

"What was that about?" asked Fell curiously. "I mean, what have you got to do in Cheltenham?"

"I thought I could look for a new dress, if that's all right with you."

"Of course. Have a good time."

"Off to bed with you and try to get a good night's sleep."

"It's so hot," mourned Fell.

"This weather can't last forever. I'll clear up here. Off with you."

Fell lay awake upstairs, listening to the domestic sounds from below as Maggie washed and dried and put away the dishes. He would need to pull his weight a bit more, he thought. Maggie was doing everything. She would make a good wife. He supposed if she was keen on Peter, they'd probably get married.

His life stretched out in front of him, empty and bleak. Without Maggie, he would be so very much on his own.

Maggie did go to Cheltenham before she was due to meet Peter and went from shop to shop trying to find a dress which would make Fell look at her as a desirable woman and not as a cosy friend.

She was pleased with her new trim figure, but mourned the fact that nothing could be done to thin her legs, which were thick and stocky below the knee. At last she found a black dress which was cut lower on the bosom than anything she had ever worn before. It fitted her beautifully and was long enough in the skirt to hide her legs. She had taken the money Fell had given her, but felt guilty at paying so much. She could have bought several pretty cotton dresses for the same price.

The sight of herself in the fitting-room mirror when she tried on the black dress had depressed her. Somehow, she felt the new hairstyle and contact lenses might have transformed her a good deal from the old Maggie, but she could not see much of a transformation.

Peter was waiting outside the town hall. He was relatively

sober. "You look great," he said. "That was a good time we had the other night."

"Is your idea of a good time getting drunk and passing out?" asked Maggie curiously.

He burst out laughing and put an arm about her shoulders. "All I need is the love of a good woman to straighten me out. What does Fell think about you going out with me?"

"He doesn't mind. He thinks it's a good idea to have the press on our side," lied Maggie, who had no intention of telling Peter that Fell did not seem to care at all, and, furthermore, they were not even engaged.

"Couldn't get front seats," said Peter. "The bigger papers like the *Birmingham Mercury* and the *Gloucester Echo* have those, but here we are in the second row, so it's not too bad."

"Is there enough money around Cheltenham to pay for designer creations such as Gucci and Versace?" asked Maggie.

"Lots of money in the whole of Gloucestershire. About the richest county in England. But this show is for charity, Save the Children. Mind you, if any of these women want to buy something, they can mark it down and get it ordered in at that new boutique Femme Fatale on the Parade." Maggie looked nervously around at all the fashionably dressed women. "How much does a ticket to this show cost?" she whispered.

"One hundred pounds."

Maggie gulped. "That's an awful lot of money."

"It's all in a good cause."

There was a long catwalk running down the centre of the main room in the town hall. Just before the lights went down, Maggie thought she saw a familiar face. She scanned the room again but, with a roll of drums, the catwalk was lit up and the faces of the audience sank back into darkness.

The models strutted past. Peter scribbled furiously in a notebook, muttering to Maggie, "I'll never remember the names of these creations if I don't take notes."

"They're all in the catalogue," whispered Maggie.

"I need my own descriptions or I'll never be able to tell one photograph from another when it comes to doing the captions," said Peter. "I mean, what the hell is faille?"

Maggie sat back to enjoy the show. The outfits were not the outrageous creations usually designed only to catch the headlines at the Paris shows, but beautiful designs which got round after round of applause. The models pouted and swayed. There was one model who looked about fourteen years old. She was thin to the point of emaciation. Her arms and legs were like sticks, and her collarbones jutted out.

What a world, marvelled Maggie, when they are dropping like flies from starvation in Africa, and yet that anorexic little girl is wearing a dress the price of which could probably feed a whole orphanage for quite a time.

At last the show finished. The photographer joined them. "Better get back with this, Peter."

"No time for a drink?"

"No," said the photographer.

"What about this evening, Maggie?" asked Peter.

"I'm going out with Fell," said Maggie, shuddering at the thought of another evening watching Peter getting drunk.

"I'll phone you."

Maggie stood on the steps of the town hall blinking in the sunlight. Then she walked towards the Parade. May as well have a look at the boutique, Femme Fatale.

Cheltenham is a Regency town, with one beautiful street of white stuccoed houses after another.

The Parade boasts the most expensive shops.

Maggie found the shop, Femme Fatale, and went inside. She looked at a few price labels and then shot out again. Even if she won the lottery, would she ever contemplate paying that much for one dress?

She walked to the car park and then drove home, wishing she had the courage to persuade Fell to take her out for dinner in the French restaurant so that she could wear her new dress.

But when she got home and had answered Fell's questions about the show, he said, "I'm getting my courage back. I think we should go to Johnny Tremp's again this evening and keep watch."

"All right," said Maggie weakly.

So they spent a long evening watching Johnny Tremp's bungalow, but no one came in and no one went out.

"Maybe we'd be better to risk the wrath of the villagers and go back and snoop around during the day," said Fell as they drove back home.

"I s'pose," said Maggie. "Did I tell you I bought a new dress today?"

"Nice?"

"Bit of an extravagance, actually. Black and slinky and only to be worn in the evening."

"Then we'd better give it an airing. We'll take a break and go to the French restaurant." The French restaurant was actually called Chez Nous, but the locals had just called it "the French restaurant" ever since it had opened in Buss five years before.

"You are good to me, Fell," said Maggie.

"You saved my life."

"I don't want your gratitude, Fell."

"But you've got it. Something's happened to me. I'm not frightened any more."

"That's good." Maggie laughed. "If you're not frightened, then I'm not frightened."

She parked the car outside the house, feeling, as they went in and reset the burglar alarm, that for the first time in her life she was really coming home. Then the miserable thought struck her that this was only a temporary arrangement. A strangled sob escaped her.

"Why, Maggie!" said Fell. "You're upset."

He put an arm around Maggie's shoulders. She moved quickly away. "I'm all right, really," she said. "Delayed shock, I think. Let's take a drink into the sitting room and have a nightcap before we go to bed."

Jerry Grange and Wayne Baxter were sloping along the road which led past Fell's house. They were two of the most unsavoury examples of Buss youth.

"You told me the old boy lived alone," complained Jerry again. Wayne had told him that Fred Flint was an easy target, old and crippled. So they had broken their way in by smashing a glass panel in the garden door, only to be met by the sight of Dottie Flint coming down the stairs with a shotgun in her hand. They had fled in terror and had hidden out under the Mayor Bridge, hearing the sound of police cars racing over their heads.

They had waited until the coast was clear and then had begun to make their way into town.

Wayne moodily tried the handles of parked cars as they walked along. A car radio might get them enough for some drugs. Outside Fell's house, he tried the handle of Maggie's car.

To his surprise it opened. He turned to Jerry with a grin on his face. "They've even left the keys in the ignition. Let's go for a spin."

They both climbed in, Wayne in the driver's seat and Jerry next to him in the passenger seat. Wayne glanced in the driving-mirror. Down the long road behind them, he saw the flashing blue light of a police car.

"Christ! The filth!" he said, and turned the ignition key.

There was a great roar as the whole car exploded in flames, shattering the night silence, blowing in the windows of Fell's house and Mrs. Moule's house next door.

Then all was still again, apart from the occasional sound of tinkling glass as another shard of Fell's broken windows dropped out.

The police car stopped. A policeman ran up with a fire extinguisher while his partner called for help.

One by one, shocked people began to emerge from the houses. Fell and Maggie in their dressing gowns stood white-faced on the front step.

"That was my car," said Maggie, turning her face into Fell's shoulder. "My car. I left the keys in my car. That was meant for us, Fell."

The street was filling up with fire engines and more police cars.

And then, appearing among the flashing blue lights, the bulk of Dunwiddy emerged.

He walked up to Fell and Maggie and then turned and surveyed the burnt-out shell of the car. He turned back. "Yours?" he asked them.

"Yes, mine," said Maggie through white lips. "That must have been meant for us."

"Could be," he said. "We'll see. Let's go inside." He signalled to another detective. "This is Detective Sergeant McIndoe. Can we go inside?"

"Careful, Maggie," cautioned Fell, supporting her inside. "There's broken glass everywhere."

They went into the sitting room. The thick curtains had been drawn and had stopped most of the window glass from flying into the room.

Dunwiddy began the questioning. Where had they been that evening? Fell and Maggie exchanged a look. "We were just driving around," said Fell. "We drove over in the direction of Moreton and then around the villages."

"Why?"

"The heat," said Maggie. "We had the windows of the car rolled down trying to get a breeze."

"And when did you get back here?"

"It must have been around eleven o'clock," said Fell. "We had a drink and then we went to bed."

"I left the keys in the ignition," said Maggie. "I've never done that before."

"We think we know who might have been in the car," said Dunwiddy. "We were looking for a couple of youths who broke into Fred Flint's. Know Fred Flint?"

"Yes," said Fell. "We visited him, about the train robbery."

"So we come back to the train robbery again. Nothing major happens in this town for years and then you pair start poking around in an old crime and all hell breaks loose. What did you get out of Fred Flint?"

"Nothing but a lot of boring railway reminiscences."

"You sure?" Sharply.

"Look," said Fell, putting his arm around Maggie, "we've

both had a bad shock. We need to get someone to board up the windows until we find a glazier. Can't this wait until the morning?"

"Just a few more questions."

Dunwiddy plodded on, taking them back through everything again. At last he said, "It seems as if someone thinks you pair are a lot brighter than you really are. I'll be back tomorrow."

Fell said suddenly, "Do we have to be here?"

"What do you mean? You can't leave the country."

"I meant, as long as we give you our address, can we go off to a hotel nearby, not too far away?"

"Don't see anything wrong with that. Come round to the station in the morning and we'll take your statements."

"Right," said Fell. "I'll see you out."

As he opened the door, he was met by the glare of television lights and camera flashes. He quickly retreated and shut the door. Maggie was going through the business phone directory. "What are you doing?" asked Fell.

"There's emergency repair services in here, glaziers, things like that. I'll get the windows fixed right away. And I'll phone the security in the morning to make sure the burglar alarm is still working."

"That's the press," said Fell, listening to the hammering at the door.

Maggie picked up the phone. "Were you serious about going away?"

"Yes, just for a few days, until the fuss dies down."

Maggie spoke into the phone urgently. Then she replaced the receiver and said with a shaky smile, "One very sleepy glazier on his road round. He has a mobile phone. I told him to call us from outside the house, so we can let him in and not the press."

It was a sleepless night. The glazier and two assistants put new glass in the windows, and then Fell told him to repair Mrs. Moule's windows next door and that he would pay for it. "Poor old thing probably doesn't have insurance," he said. Fell and Maggie both worked busily, cleaning up glass from the floors. Then they both got washed and dressed and packed suitcases.

"Where are we going?" asked Maggie.

"We'll find a hotel in Moreton," said Fell. "We'll try the White Hart Royal and then we'll find out more about Johnny Tremp. I'm sure he's the villain. We check up on him and the next thing you know, someone tries to kill us."

After the alarm system had been checked in the morning, Fell called a taxi to take them to the police station. They fought their way to the taxi through a barrage of reporters' questions. "Was it the IRA?" called some. "Come on, Maggie," yelled Peter. "Give me a break."

But they finally got into the cab and were driven off.

At the police station, Dunwiddy took them through everything again. "Do you know why the car blew up?" asked Fell.

"They're still working on it, but they think it might be Semtex."

"But that's a terrorists' weapon!"

"Exactly. And I have been answering questions from Scotland Yard as to whether you pair have any connection with Northern Ireland."

"That's ridiculous," exclaimed Fell. "I've only been out of

Buss once and that was recently when we went to London for the day."

"So where will you be staying?"

"Only as far as Moreton-in-Marsh. I was hoping the White Hart Royal might have a couple of rooms."

Dunwiddy pushed a phone forward. "Phone now."

Fell phoned. He was told he was lucky that they had just received two cancellations.

Separate rooms, thought Dunwiddy. What an old-fashioned couple.

"Now," said Fell, "is there any way we can get out of here and avoid the press?"

"I'll get you a driver to take you to Moreton. Hide down in the back seat and he'll drive you straight out."

At the Moreton hotel, Maggie left her suitcase on the bed and went to Fell's room which was next to her own. She sat down on the bed and suddenly burst into tears. "We're safe here," said Fell, putting his arms around her. "Poor Maggie. Look, I'll drop the whole thing. Forget about the damn robbery."

Maggie dried her eyes. "It's not that," she said shakily. "I'm being silly. It's my little car. When I was living with Mother, it was the only place I felt free and safe. It was my own little tin world."

"We'll rent one."

"It costs so much to rent one, Fell. There's a garage just outside of town. I saw it when we drove past. They've got second-hand cars for sale. I phoned the insurance company before I left. My car wasn't worth anything, but they are sending an assessor to look at the wreck and they'll pay up quite quickly."

"Okay, we'll go and get a car and then have some sleep."

They bought an old Rover at a garage which had a range of second-hand cars. "I would have taken something smaller and cheaper," said Maggie, as she drove off.

"It's a nice red," said Fell naively, for he knew nothing about cars. "I like the colour of this one."

"I hope it lasts. It's got more than one hundred thousand miles on the clock."

"We're mobile, anyway. Let's go back and get some sleep."

Fell woke Maggie at seven in the evening. She bathed and changed and then they both went down for dinner.

"Let's leave our spying on Tremp for tonight," said Fell.

"All right," said Maggie, relieved. "But don't you think we should tell Dunwiddy about Tremp? I mean, why not?"

"We've left it a bit late. He'll say, why didn't we tell him before?"

"I suppose so," said Maggie reluctantly. "And we should have told him about the attempt on your life when you were pushed in the river. Aren't you frightened, Fell?"

"Not yet. It's odd, but I seem to be moving in a strange world where the unacceptable has become acceptable."

"So we go on?"

"Yes, we go on."

EIGHT

†

IN the morning, before they could set out, they were visited by two men from the Special Branch. The questions began again. Had either of them ever been in Northern Ireland? Had they any Irish relatives? Neither had, which was unusual; a great proportion of the populace of the British Isles having Irish ancestry somewhere in their family tree.

"I really don't think the IRA would bother with a little market town like Buss," said Fell.

"They hide out all over the place on the mainland," said one of the men. "Ten years ago, a lodging house over on the other side of Buss was raided, and bomb-making equipment, guns, and a quantity of Semtex were seized. That's all for now. But if you plan on changing your address, let the police know."

Then Dunwiddy phoned. He said that they should let him know when they planned to return and a police guard would be put on Fell's house. "In that case," Fell said, "we might go back tomorrow."

He and Maggie drove off to Bramley-on-the-Hedges. "Instead of parking outside the house," said Fell, "we'll park right outside the village stores and see if we can spot him in the village."

"And what good will that do?" asked Maggie nervously.

"I want him worried," said Fell. "I'm getting very angry at the attempt on our lives."

After an hour, a little group of villagers began to gather outside the shop, staring angrily at Fell and Maggie, who were parked on the opposite side of the road.

"I don't get it," said Fell. "Why are they so hostile?"

"I don't know." Maggie looked nervously at them. "You know, Fell, I wish we had told Dunwiddy about someone trying to push you in the river. I wish we had confided in him more."

"I know," said Fell. "But I was so worried about that Andy Briggs business. I still am. They'll have been questioning and questioning the neighbours, and I'm scared that one of them might remember seeing someone like Andy. Oh, God, what if old Mrs. Moule chatters on about us doing the garden in the middle of the night and they start searching the garden and find the cash box? Think of the questions. Then old Mrs. Wakeham will need to tell them about the money, and everyone will know I'm a bastard and the tax people will be after me. You know, there's been quite a few stories in the newspapers about some householder or another surprising a burglar and hitting him over the head and ending up in court themselves, charged with assault."

"One of them's coming over," hissed Maggie.

A powerful-looking woman with a chiffon scarf tied over a head full of rollers was bearing down on them.

"People like you are a disgrace," she hissed. "Why can't you leave poor Mr. Tremp alone? You lot are like jackals. If you want money, then go out and work for it."

"I don't know what you're talking about," said Maggie.

"Just because he's won the lottery doesn't mean he should pay out to every layabout."

"The lottery!" exclaimed Fell.

"Don't act the innocents with me. The poor man was hounded by people looking for a handout. He thought he was free of them. We don't want your sort in this village."

"Actually," lied Fell, "we don't know what you are talking about. We're looking for a place to stay and we thought this village would be a nice place. We've changed our minds. Drive on, Maggie."

With relief, Maggie shot off. They drove in silence and then Maggie stopped at the side of the road. "The lottery!" she said. "Do you believe it?"

"They believe it, anyway," said Fell. "Wait a bit. If he was so plagued by people wanting money from him, his win must have been in the papers. What about phoning Peter?"

"Oh, he'll want a story from us."

"So we'll give him a story, Maggie. We've been interviewed by the police so many times that one more interview won't matter."

Peter, in answer to Maggie's phone call, arrived at the hotel accompanied by a photographer.

Maggie talked to the manager, who said they could use the

little residents' lounge on the ground floor. Peter cast a longing glance in the direction of the bar across the hall, but got down to the interview. Fell and Maggie were sitting together on the sofa. At one point during the questioning, Fell took Maggie's hand in his. Maggie held his hand tightly. Peter looked at their joined hands and scowled, but the story was too important to let personal feelings interfere with it and so he pressed on.

When he had finished and photographs had been taken, Maggie asked him if he had found out anything about Johnny Tremp's lottery win.

"Yes, it was in the *Courier* two years ago," said Peter. "Eight people won, each getting a little over a million pounds. Johnny was one of them. Why ask? Did you think he had decided to blossom out all those years after the robbery and spend some of his ill-gotten gains?"

"Something like that," said Fell ruefully. "But don't put it in your story."

"It's all right. I've got enough without using it. Anyway, Johnny has the reputation of being a nasty character. He'd probably sue you for defamation of character. Maggie, can I have a word?"

Maggie and Peter walked outside the hotel. "I didn't realize you pair were so close," said Peter huffily.

Maggie could still feel the warm clasp of Fell's hand. "We were going through a bad patch, but we're all right now," she said.

"So no hope for me?"

"I'm afraid not, Peter."

"Oh, well, that's life." He put his arms around her and kissed her full on the mouth. "Remember me if it comes unstuck."

Fell saw the embrace and felt a pain deep inside him. It struck him just how much he had come to rely on Maggie's company, on her warmth and strength and sympathy. It was only fair to urge Maggie to tell Peter that their engagement was a sham.

When she came back into the hotel, he really meant to tell her, but she said, "What will we do now?"

He replied, "I think we should phone Dunwiddy and tell him we're going home." And instead of saying she should now tell Peter that the engagement was off, he found himself saying, "We need some relaxation. And you haven't worn your new dress. After I've phoned Dunwiddy, I'll phone the French restaurant and make a reservation for this evening."

When they got back home, a policeman was already on duty outside the house. Maggie made him coffee and took it out to him. Fell could see her chatting and laughing with the policeman. It seemed incredible that such a short time ago he would have been delighted to be rid of Maggie.

He would not admit to himself when she came back indoors that his next suggestion was prompted by a desire to keep her with him as long as possible. "I think we should take a break from all our worries and get a builder in to see if we can make a new kitchen," he said.

"Good idea," said Maggie. "Will you need permission from the council for the alteration?"

"I shouldn't think so. Instead of knocking down a wall, we could keep the old kitchen and just use it as a scullery. That way we could avoid planning permission."

"You've got letters there? Aren't you going to read them?"

Fell picked up the letters and sat down and flipped through

them. They were from his relatives. One, from his Aunt Agnes, blamed Maggie for the whole thing, saying she had thought that Maggie looked like "one of them terrorists."

The others, from Tom and Barbara and Fred, said pretty much all the same thing, and that his sainted parents would be turning in their graves.

"Not one word of sympathy!" said Fell, throwing them down in disgust. "You would think nearly getting blown up was my fault." He looked bleakly at the letters scattered on the floor.

"Better phone them up and tell them you're all right," said Maggie.

"Why? I bet all I'd get is a load of recriminations."

"I'm weary. I think I'll have a bath and an hour's sleep." Maggie got to her feet. "I just want to switch off. We've got the evening to look forward to."

"The box!" exclaimed Fell. "I'd better have a look in the garden and make sure the police haven't dug it up."

He headed for the garden. "If they had," Maggie called after him, "they would have told us right away."

Fell looked uneasily at the patch where the box was buried. Nothing seemed to have been disturbed.

"Coo-ee! Mr. Dolphin!"

Fell jumped nervously.

"I'm up here."

Fell turned round and located the source of the voice. He could see a little of old Mrs. Moule's face peering through the branches of a tree. So that was how she had seen him the night when they thought they had been digging a grave for Andy Briggs.

"I just want to thank you for my windows," she called.

"Least I could do."

"Thanks anyway. Bring your young lady in for tea sometime."

"Will do."

The face retreated. Fell looked thoughtfully at where the cash box was buried. At least, with his inheritance safely in the bank, he would not need to use the cash box. Still, he wished he could dig it up and put it somewhere he could get at it without being observed.

He went back into the house He could hear Maggie running a bath upstairs. He thought he would follow her example by catching some sleep.

He went up to his room and looked around. Before he decided on a new kitchen, he should really redecorate this room. It reminded him of Mr. and Mrs. Dolphin and of his unhappy childhood. Perhaps he and Maggie could forget about this wretched train robbery and concentrate on getting the whole house liveable. Maggie would know what to do. But Maggie might not be around for much longer, judging by the way Peter had kissed her.

Fell was waiting in the sitting room that evening when Maggie came in. She was wearing the new black dress. The low-cut neckline showed off the tops of a pair of full and firm white breasts. Maggie was wearing her contact lenses and her hair shone in the lamplight.

"What do you think?" she asked, pirouetting in front of him.

"Fine, but the neckline's a bit low."

"Oh." Maggie's face fell with disappointment. "Should I wear something else?"

"No, no, you look great. I don't know why I said that. It's just . . . funny . . . I don't know. I haven't been in the way of thinking of you as a woman. I mean . . ."

"I know what you mean," said Maggie stiffly. "Shall we go?"

†

Maggie's hand hovered over the ignition in the car and then dropped. "I'm frightened to switch it on."

The policeman on guard came over. "Anything wrong, miss?" he asked, leaning in the open window. He was looking right down Maggie's cleavage, thought Fell crossly.

"Silly," said Maggie. "I'm frightened of another bomb."

"No one's touched that car while you've been inside, miss, but release the hood and I'll check inside. Then you'll feel all right."

He inspected the engine, then he crawled underneath the car, emerging finally to give Maggie a beaming smile. "All clear."

"Oh, thank you. You are kind," said Maggie. She and the policeman smiled warmly at each other.

"Can we go?" demanded Fell testily. As Maggie let in the clutch and moved off, Fell added, "There's no need to go overboard, Maggie. He's only doing his job."

"He's nice."

"If you say so," said Fell grumpily. Maggie should stay plain Maggie and not go around flaunting her bosoms in a slinky black dress.

Maggie parked in the car park and they walked around to the front of the restaurant, which faced the river.

"Look," said Maggie, clutching Fell's arm and pointing to the sky.

"What?"

"A cloud. Quite a big one. Do you think the heat is going to be over at last?"

"It's bound to end soon and then we'll all be terribly British and complain about the rain."

They went into the restaurant and were given the table at the window they had had on the day that Fell had "proposed." How grateful I was then for so little, thought Maggie, and now it's not enough.

Fell stiffened and raised the menu to hide his face. Maggie twisted around. Melissa Harley was at a table over by the far wall. She was talking animatedly to a middle-aged businessman.

And then, as Maggie turned back, she thought she saw a face she recognized. Fell, cautiously lowering the menu, saw her frown.

"What's up?"

"Nothing. I thought I recognized someone, but I haven't a good memory for faces."

"It's Melissa."

"I know. I saw her. It's not her, it's a blonde woman at a table along from her."

Fell looked across the restaurant. "I think that's Inspector Rudfern's daughter, but I'm not sure. Let's choose something to eat."

They ordered salad and Dover sole and a bottle of white wine. "I'm surprised your mother hasn't phoned or been round," said Fell.

"She's like that. I mean, I'm not usually the target of attempted murder, but I don't think she cares much."

"Did your father die a long time ago?"

A painful blush crept up Maggie's face. "I don't know who my father was," she said, "and I don't think Mum knows either."

"Oh, Maggie," said Fell sadly. "What a pair we are. It's a good thing we've got each other."

She brightened. "Yes, isn't it?"

"What about Peter? Do you think you'll marry him?"

"I don't think I'll be seeing Peter again. But you've got Melissa."

"I may as well tell you, Maggie, you were right all along. She was only interested in my money. Now it looks as if she's getting to work on another sucker. Dreams are funny things. I saw a beautiful woman and she wasn't really beautiful at all."

"It must have been a terrible shock," said Maggie. "Were you dreadfully hurt?"

"I felt silly and ashamed of myself."

"How did you find out?"

"The lawyer warned me against her. I didn't want to believe him, but after I met her and talked to her, it became all too obvious what she was after. There was nothing there but greed. What happened with Peter? I thought you looked very affectionate today."

"Peter was being affectionate. I wasn't. He was kissing me farewell. I had just told him I wouldn't be seeing him again."

"Why?"

"He's nice. But he does drink rather a lot." Maggie told him what had really happened at the disco.

They discussed the weird ways of coincidence while they both grew more relaxed and happier.

Then they began to reminisce about their days in the Palace Hotel, laughing over the antics of some of the more difficult customers. Melissa Harley left, but Fell was barely aware of her.

At last, when they had finished their coffee, Fell said, "Home?"

And Maggie agreed happily. "Home."

†

There was a new policeman on duty, a grumpy-looking man. He nodded to them. "I'll bring you out a cup of tea and some biscuits," said Maggie.

The policeman smiled. "That's very kind of you, miss."

"You do fuss over them, Maggie."

"I'm grateful he's standing guard." But Fell obscurely thought that Maggie should not be fussing around arranging a tray of tea and biscuits for a constable while wearing that low-necked dress.

Then he could hear her chatting to the policeman and the policeman's laugh. Well, he wasn't going to wait up for her. He would be glad when she appeared in the morning looking more like her usual self. And Fell would not admit to himself that he wanted the old frumpy Maggie back, and not this one who seemed to be attracting men.

The next day, Fell, pleased to see Maggie in a print cotton dress and with her thick glasses back on, standing over the stove making scrambled eggs, told her he would like to smarten up the bedrooms first.

"The beds are awful and old and lumpy," he complained.

Maggie deftly served scrambled eggs and toast. "We could be extravagant," she said. "We could call one of those small cheap removal firms and get the old beds taken away to the dump today. Have you bagged up the stuff in your mother's bedroom?"

"Yes, but it's still in garbage bags on the bedroom floor."

"Then they can take those as well and drop them off at Oxfam. What about the wardrobes?"

"Let's get rid of them as well. We'll get new beds today and then strip the walls and paint them."

"Grand. The minute we're finished breakfast, we'll get to work."

Later that day, with a dust sheet over his new bed, Fell worked away happily, stripping wallpaper from his bedroom. He could hear Maggie whistling tunelessly as she worked in her room. This was the life, he thought. Forget about that damned robbery. All he wanted now was peace and safety.

"Maggie!" he called.

"Mmm?"

"I've just had an idea. Why don't we phone up the *Courier* and say that we're leaving any investigations into the train robbery to the police? That way, whoever it is out there will know we're no longer a threat."

Maggie appeared in the doorway. "You mean, give up the whole thing?"

"Why not? I'm hopeless, Maggie. I haven't got a clue who might have done it. Look at the mistake I made with Johnny Tremp."

"Well, the police do have all the resources and that attempt on our lives has opened up the whole case again. I'll phone Whittaker, if you like."

"Tell you what; we'll have a break and go and see him."

Tommy Whittaker was in his office. "That was a good story," he said, handing over a copy of the *Courier*.

"We want to give you another story," said Fell, ignoring the newspaper. He told the editor how they had planned to drop all their investigations.

"Pity about that," said the editor. "It rather caught the local imagination."

"It's not like in books," said Fell earnestly. "Amateurs like us don't have the expertise of the police and in fact we might just be complicating matters for them."

"You're not just saying this to make sure there won't be any more attempts on your lives?"

"Well, of course," said Maggie. "That's a good part of it. What we mean is why should we go on risking our lives when we know now we're never going to find a solution?"

"I'm grateful to you for today's exclusive, so we'll run your story."

"Thanks," said Fell. "Now we can get on with our lives."

Tommy grinned. "I suppose the next story we'll be covering will be your wedding."

Maggie blushed and looked down.

"Set the date yet?"

"Not yet," said Fell.

"Let me know."

When they left the newspaper office, there was a new constraint between them. "Back to housework," said Fell at last. "You don't think I'm weak to drop it?"

"No, Fell, you're not weak and neither am I. We just want to stay alive."

The cloud Maggie had seen had not been joined by others. In the following week, while they both shopped and worked and painted, a haze covered the sky but the heat was as stifling as ever.

At the end of the week, he was just finishing painting the bedroom walls when Fell called to Maggie, who was working in her room, "Do we have a spare newspaper? I want to put some sheets on the floor in case the paint drips."

"It's supposed to be non-drip paint," Maggie called back. "I'll have a look."

She went down to the kitchen. They had not been buying any newspapers. There were only two: the edition of the *Courier* that Tommy Whittaker had given them and the new issue carrying the story that they had both given up the hunt. She would ask Fell if he wanted to keep them as souvenirs.

Then she remembered the fashion show she had gone to with Peter. Had anything appeared? She had read only the stories about themselves. She opened the copy with the story on the front page, which had appeared after they had been interviewed at the hotel.

Inside was a double spread of photographs. Maggie looked at them. There was one dress, a Versace model. She studied it closely, something tugging at her memory. Then she went slowly up the stairs, holding the newspaper.

"Fell," she said, going into his room, "there's something odd here."

"What?"

Maggie sat down on the bed. She opened the newspaper at the double spread of fashion photographs. "Do you see this dress?"

Fell sat down beside her. "Yes. Versace, it says. What about it?"

"I was looking at this photo and then I remembered I'd seen that dress recently."

"Of course you had, silly. At the fashion show."

"No, last night. Inspector Rudfern's daughter was wearing

one just like it. And another thing. I told you I have a bad memory for faces, but just before the lights went down at the fashion show, I saw her. I'm now sure it was her."

"So, Maggie, what's this got to do with anything?"

"Don't you see?" said Maggie slowly. "It's a bit odd if a retired police inspector's daughter can afford a Versace dress."

"Meaning Inspector Rudfern masterminded the robbery himself? Come on, Maggie. Him of all people."

"But Fell, how could she afford a dress like that? It costs a few thousand. I'm sure."

"As much as that!"

"For an original, yes."

"Wait a bit, Maggie. I read somewhere that chain stores sometimes buy the pattern and run up something like it."

"You're probably right," said Maggie with a sigh. "I'd better get back to work. Do you want to use these newspapers or keep them?"

"I'll use them. I don't want to be reminded of anything now to do with the robbery."

"Right. I'll get back to work as well."

Fell began to paint again. Imagine if it were old Rudfern, he thought, amused. Imagine an old man like that creeping down the street at night to put Semtex in Maggie's car. And then he remembered uneasily those men from the Special Branch saying there had been a raid on a house in Buss and among other things a quantity of Semtex had been seized. When had it been? Ten years ago, that was it. Of course it was all mad, but if Rudfern had still been in the police force, then he was ideally situated to get his hands on Semtex.

He smiled and shook his head and began to paint again.

But the thought of Rudfern nagged and nagged at his mind. At last he threw down the brush and called to Maggie, "Feel like taking a break and having a drink?"

Maggie's voice came back to him. "Great idea. My arms are getting tired."

When they were relaxing in the sitting room over glasses of gin and tonic, Fell swirled the ice cubes round in his glass and said cautiously, "You know, Maggie, I've been thinking."

"What about?"

"About Rudfern."

Maggie's heart sank. She wished she had never mentioned anything. She wanted to forget about robbery and murder and mayhem for the rest of her life.

"I was just being silly. Of course she must have been wearing a cheap copy."

"I mean, it was just a show for charity, wasn't it? I mean, they weren't taking orders, were they?"

"People could order things," said Maggie reluctantly. "There's a deadly expensive boutique in the Parade called Femme Fatale. You could order what you wanted from the show through them. I went into Femme Fatale. I took a look at some of their ready-to-wear stuff and was shocked at the prices."

"There's something else," said Fell. "Semtex. Those men from London, they said a house in Buss had been raided ten years ago and the police had found Semtex then. Who better to get his hands on the stuff than someone in the police force?"

"I don't think that can be the case," said Maggie. "I mean, just suppose by the wildest flight of the imagination that it was Rudfern. Why would he suddenly decide to pinch some explosive like Semtex, thinking this might come in handy someday?"

Fell bit his lip. Drop it, pleaded Maggie's mind. Let's be safe. Let's go back to playing house.

"We could start tomorrow by going to that boutique in Cheltenham and finding out if a Miss Rudfern . . . Is she married?"

"I don't know," said Maggie, "but I shouldn't think so. She's obviously living with her father. Of course there may be a husband somewhere in that villa, or there may be an ex."

"I wish I knew where to start, apart from that boutique," fretted Fell. "We can hardly watch their house."

Maggie wanted to shout with frustration, "You said we should give up!" But instead she said, "We've got a new second-hand car. If they saw the old one, they won't recognize the new one. But even if we watch, what are we going to see? The robbery was so long ago and the other people who were involved in it will either be dead or gone off somewhere."

"True," agreed Fell. "So we'll go to Cheltenham in the morning."

The haze which had covered the sky above for the last week had thickened into a uniform grey as they drove over the Worcestershire border and into neighbouring Gloucestershire. "It might rain at last," said Maggie.

Everything looked so still and parched. But the trees beside the road had a waiting air about their stillness, as if they somehow knew that an end to the heat of this dandelion summer was near.

Maggie found a parking place outside the town hall and together they walked around the corner and down into the Parade.

"How should we go about this?" asked Fell as they stood outside the shop. "I mean, we can't just ask bluntly, 'Did a woman called Miss Rudfern buy a Versace dress from you?' "

"We could say we worked for her. I could say I was her housekeeper," said Maggie, "and that she had complained about there being a loose thread near the hem."

"Won't the assistant or manager or whoever recognize us from our photo in the newspaper?"

"It was just in the *Buss Courier* and I'm sure no one in Cheltenham bothers looking at that."

"But we were on television on the night the car blew up."

Maggie stood and thought hard. She now wanted to find out if Inspector Rudfern's daughter had bought that expensive dress. With any luck, it would turn out she had not and then they could forget about the whole thing.

"I think," she said slowly, "that no one is going to connect us with the couple on television, not if we say we're working for the Rudferns. People don't often recognize people if they're not in the setting they expect them to be."

"All right. We'll try it."

They both walked into the shop. A woman in a tailored black dress approached them. Maggie judged her to be French, because she had a hard middle-aged face and yet exuded an air of sexiness. Maggie had served French tourists when she had worked at the Palace and had noticed that even the plainest of the women managed to have an air of femininity, a certain allure.

"Can I help you?"

Yes, she did have a slight French accent.

"We are employed by a Miss Rudfern who lives in Buss,"

began Maggie. "After the fashion show at the town hall, she ordered a gold faille Versace gown from you. She says the stitching at the hem is loose and when I said I was going to Cheltenham, she asked me to drop in and talk to you about it."

"Rudfern? I do not recall the name. I'll check the books."

The woman went into the back shop and came out with a leather-bound ledger. She opened it and ran a long finger ending in a scarlet nail, so long it curved like a claw, down the pages. "Ah, I thought so. No Rudfern. I only sold one Versace gown in gold faille to a Mrs. Lewis, a Mrs. Gloria Lewis."

"I'm sorry to have wasted your time," said Maggie. "My employer must have mistaken the shop."

She closed the book again, looking bored. "Exactly."

They had just reached the door of the shop when Fell turned back and said, "Where does this Mrs. Lewis live?"

The Frenchwoman clicked her tongue impatiently but opened the ledger again. Strange, thought Maggie. A less expensive shop would almost certainly have a computer, but with prices like these, probably so few were sold that . . .

"Buss," said the woman. "She lives in Buss."

"May we have her address?" asked Fell.

Her hard face hardened even more. "No, of course you may not. Who are you anyway? I do not like thees." Her accent had become more marked. "Are you the reporters?"

"No, no," said Fell, taking Maggie's arm and hustling her out of the shop.

They walked rapidly a little way up the Parade and then Fell stopped and said, "It could be her."

"So how do we find out?" asked Maggie.

"Tommy Whittaker."

"But if he thinks we suspect Rudfern," wailed Maggie, "he'll maybe poke his nose in and if Rudfern gets to hear of it, he might sue us."

"We'll take him for a drink." Fell's eyes were shining with excitement. "We'll get him talking about this and that and slip in a few questions."

Maggie felt weary. Her cotton dress was sticking to her body and she knew her hair was lank. In her heart she hoped the editor would be too busy to talk to them.

It was with relief that Maggie heard the receptionist at the *Buss Courier* telling Fell about an hour later that Mr. Whittaker was out for lunch.

"So that's that," said Maggie cheerfully. "I'm all hot and sticky. Let's go home and—"

"Lunch," interrupted Fell. "That means a liquid lunch. Let's try the Red Lion."

Maggie trailed beside him along the street past the Georgian front of the courthouse to the Red Lion. She noticed with a feeling of resignation Tommy Whittaker sitting at a table by the window. He hailed them cheerfully and asked them to get their drinks and bring him a double Scotch.

When they were seated around the table, Tommy looked at them and asked, "Found out anything?"

"I'm not looking for anything," replied Fell. "We thought we would find you here. We thought we would drop in and thank you for putting that story in that we'd given up."

"And have you?"

"Definitely. What on earth can we do that the police can't?"

"I dunno," said Tommy, "but they didn't do much of a good job at the beginning, if you ask me."

"Did Inspector Rudfern have a bad reputation?" asked Maggie.

"On the contrary. A good copper, rising steadily up the ranks, working hard. Usually cooperated well with the press, but not on this one. Wouldn't give us a morsel."

"Maybe he didn't have anything to give?" suggested Fell.

"It looks that way."

"He certainly didn't seem very enthusiastic when we met him," said Maggie.

"Grumpy old bugger." Tommy took a gulp of whisky.

"His daughter's pretty grumpy as well," said Fell. "What's her name again?"

"Oh, her, Gloria Lewis."

Maggie felt a jolt in her stomach.

"She got soured a long time ago," Tommy was going on. "I'll tell you about it. Goodness, I've got an empty glass."

"I'll get you another." Fell went to the bar, but it took some time, as the barman seemed determined to ignore him. When he got back to the table, it was to find Maggie on her own. "Where is he?"

"Gone to the loo."

"What did he say about Gloria Lewis?"

"He said he'd tell us both." Tommy emerged from the loo and then infuriatingly stopped to talk to various locals. Impatiently Fell held up the glass of whisky. Tommy saw it, ended his conversation, and came hurrying up. He raised the glass, took a gulp, and then sat down. "Ah, that's better. Where was I?"

"Gloria Lewis," prompted Maggie.

"Her, yes. She got married to James Lewis, a high-flyer."

"A high-flyer in *Buss,*" exclaimed Maggie.

Tommy laughed. "No, London man, much older than she was. Must have been about nineteen and he was forty. Owned a chain of restaurants. Was thinking of opening a restaurant in Buss. Checked in at the Palace. Called in at the cop shop to find out if it was a safe area and got to know Rudfern. Rudfern invited him home. He fell for Gloria. She used to be quite a looker, by all accounts. Whirlwind romance, got married, off to London. One month later, he's got his eye on a blonde model and he's bored with Gloria. Gloria, furious at his indifference, has an affair with one of his friends to teach him a lesson. Friend tells James. James sues for divorce as injured party. No children. Gloria gets zilch. Rich lifestyle goes down the pan, back to being copper's daughter in Buss."

"She must have hated giving up the high life," said Maggie.

"I s'pose."

"Didn't want to marry again?"

"I don't think she found anyone around here good enough for her. I gather you were asking young Peter about Johnny Tremp."

"It turned out to be a dead end," said Fell.

"Still," said Tommy, "it could have been a good lead. It must have looked to you as if he'd sat on that money all these years and then decided to spend it when everything had cooled down."

"It did seem that way." Fell noticed Tommy's glass was empty again. The pub was very hot and smelly and he now wanted to escape and talk over with Maggie what they had learned. Then it struck him that Gloria might have money of her own, and who better to tell them than Tommy. "Another drink?" he asked.

"Very kind," beamed Tommy.

"I'll get it." Maggie pushed back her chair. "What about you, Fell?"

"Another gin and tonic."

When Maggie left for the bar, Fell said as casually as he could, "Does Gloria Lewis have a business of some kind?"

"Her business is looking after the old man."

Maggie returned with the drinks. "That was quick," said Fell. "How did you manage it? I thought that barman would never serve me."

"An attractive lady will always get served first," said Tommy, leering at Maggie.

Fell thought crossly that no one could call Maggie attractive on that hot day. Her face was shiny and her hair limp. "I believe you gave our Peter the elbow," Tommy was saying.

"I am engaged," said Maggie.

"Poor chap thought he was in there with a chance. Quite cut up, he is," teased Tommy.

"Then he should know better than to try to poach on someone else's land," said Fell sharply, and Maggie looked at him in such amazement that Fell actually blushed.

Tommy's eyes now focused on Fell. "You've got an odd engagement. I mean, what was Peter to think? You were wining and dining with Melissa Harley."

"That was different. That was business."

"Didn't get any money out of you, did she?"

"No."

"Just as well. Terrible woman. Probably thought you were an easy mark, but I'll bet your young lady here wasn't as easily fooled."

"Nor was Fell," said Maggie loyally.

"Mind you," said Tommy, "I told Peter I didn't think he

had a chance. You always looked very much like a couple to me."

"Are you working on any good stories at the moment?" asked Maggie, desperate to change the subject.

Tommy shook his head. "You two have provided the best stories we've had in years. It's back to school-sports days and flower-arrangement classes."

"We've got to go," said Fell. Tommy looked settled in the pub for the afternoon.

"Okay. Be a pal and send another double over on your way out."

"What a sponge!" complained Maggie as they stood at the bar. Fell signalled to the barman, who ignored him.

"Service, please!" shouted Maggie. The barman sulkily served them. Fell carried the drink to Tommy, said goodbye, and then joined Maggie, who was waiting by the door. "Let's get home," he said.

They walked back to the High Street where Maggie had parked the car and drove home, Fell going over and over what they had just learned. Once home, Maggie headed for the kitchen. "I'll fix us something to eat."

"No, you won't. Go and sit down and relax. You've been doing all the cooking lately. What do you feel like eating?"

"Just a sandwich. The heat has taken my appetite away."

Fell made a plate of ham sandwiches and a pot of tea and carried the lot through to the sitting room.

There was a ring at the doorbell. Fell put down the tray and went to answer it. He was so absorbed in thoughts of Gloria Lewis that he half-expected her to be standing on the doorstep, but it was Maggie's mother.

"Going to ask me in?"

"Come in," said Fell reluctantly. "Maggie's in the sitting room."

Maggie's mother was deeply tanned. Fell thought she looked like a piece of bad-tempered old leather.

"So what's all this about?" began Mrs. Partlett as soon as she saw her daughter. "I go off to Tenerife and when I get back the town's buzzing with the news that you pair nearly got blown up by the IRA."

Maggie could not be bothered explaining about the train robbery, so she said, "Someone mistook us for someone else."

"I thought that might be it. Who's going to bother about a pair of wimps like you?"

"You are in my house and while you are here, you'll keep a civil tongue in your head," said Fell quietly.

She looked at him as amazed as if a pet rabbit had bitten her on the ankle. "Oh, well," she said with a shrug, "when are you going to get married?"

"Next month," said Fell in that same quiet voice.

"And am I invited?"

"We'll think about it."

"What! Don't you dare stop me from coming to my own daughter's wedding."

"I will do what I want. If you are going to go on sneering at Maggie, then I don't want you around."

She had been about to sit down. But instead she marched back towards the door. "You just try to stop me," she shouted. She opened the street door, walked outside and slammed it behind her.

"Oh, Fell," said Maggie mistily, "I've been longing for someone to stand up for me."

"I don't like to see you hurt. Now let's eat, Maggie, and

we'll get out some pens and paper and start working out what we've got."

If only he had meant that about marriage, thought Maggie, and bit into a ham sandwich which tasted as dry as dust.

NINE

†

THE thing is this," said Fell, making notes, "why was it so important for my father to get that shift? I know he was not my father, but I can't get out of calling him that. He was a miser. Why should he pay Terry Weale a tenner? You got anything?"

"Maybe Tommy Whittaker was wrong. Maybe Gloria got a large divorce settlement from James Lewis."

"Could be. But I can't envisage an old man like Rudfern dressing up as a postman, pushing me in the river and putting Semtex in your car."

The doorbell rang. "I'll get it," said Fell. "I'll take a look out of the window first."

He opened the sitting-room window and peered round it. Then he headed for the door, saying, "It's my aunt Agnes."

Aunt Agnes was as buttoned up and whiskery as ever. "I came to see what you were up to," she said.

"Come in," said Fell.

Maggie in the sitting room heard Aunt Agnes say crossly, "It's all the fault of that girl you're engaged to. I bet she has a criminal background."

And then she heard Fell's voice, quiet and intense, "While you are here, no criticism of Maggie at all. Of course it has nothing to do with her."

Aunt Agnes stumped into the sitting room. She eyed Maggie with disfavour. Fell followed her in.

"Nothing like this has ever happened in our family," she complained.

"But I'm not of your family, am I?" Fell said.

She goggled at Fell.

"I appear to be the son of a certain Paul Wakeham."

"How did you find that out?"

"So you knew all along," said Fell flatly.

"My sister and her husband were good parents to you. There was no need for you to know."

"On the contrary," said Fell savagely, "they were paid a large sum of money for my education. I could have got a place at university. But, oh no, they pleaded poverty as usual and I had to work as a waiter."

"It's all water under the bridge." Aunt Agnes gave an irritating sniff.

"Have you any idea of what a shock it was to me?" shouted Fell.

"It's no use you getting uppity with me, young man. My sister reared you as if you were her own."

"And you knew all along! And have you any idea what that rearing was like? The loneliness, the beatings, the constant complaining about how they couldn't afford this and they couldn't afford that."

"You aren't going to the papers with this, are you?" exclaimed Aunt Agnes. "Think of our good name."

Fell's anger left as abruptly as it had come. "No," he said wearily, "I'm as anxious to protect my reputation as you are. While you're here, you can answer me one question. Did my . . . I mean Mr. Dolphin have anything to do with the train robbery?"

"Bite your tongue! Of course not!"

"But on the day of the robbery he went on duty, even though it was his day off. He even paid Terry Weale a tenner!"

Aunt Agnes looked uncomfortable. "I 'member that day. Because of the robbery, you see. It was that Colonel Wakeham. He said he wasn't going to have nothing to do with them after you was handed over. But he suddenly says he's going to come round and see how the boy is. So Charlie says he's not having him round the house and the boy's busy and that Colonel Wakeham is to meet him at the station in the morning and he'll give him a report. He saw the colonel, and soon as the colonel had left, that was when he got the call about stopping the train. He couldn't tell the police the truth, for he had to protect you."

"Yes, and I might have found out just what a money-grabbing miser he was," said Fell bitterly.

"No need to take that tone with me," said Aunt Agnes, every hair on her face bristling with indignation. "They didn't want you. If it hadn't been for my sister, you'd have ended up in an orphanage."

"Would you like some tea?" asked Maggie, speaking for the first time.

"No, she's just leaving," said Fell. "How did you get here?"

"The train."

"I'll get you a cab. And then I don't want to see you again."

"There's gratitude for you. Shunning those that clothed you and fed you."

Fell went through and phoned for a cab. When it arrived, he went out and paid the driver. "I suppose you'll be wanting your furniture back" were Aunt Agnes's last words.

"Keep it." Fell slammed the cab door on her and returned indoors to Maggie.

"It wasn't really her fault," said Maggie awkwardly when Fell sank down in a chair and buried his face in his hands. "I mean, she didn't keep the money from you or bring you up."

Fell took his hands away from his face. "I suppose not. Let's get back to these wretched notes. The trouble about that lottery business is that Johnny Tremp is such an ideal suspect. He's a nasty bit of work and brutal enough to have been in on the robbery. All we've got is one police inspector with an expensive daughter."

Maggie was to regret her next words. "I suppose we could just go and ask him."

Fell stared at her.

Maggie laughed. "I'm being ridiculous."

"I don't know. You know, Maggie, why not? Why not just ask? We could watch the house until we see the daughter leave and get him on his own. No witnesses."

"Fell, it won't do. He'll just get angry and deny the whole thing."

"But don't you see, it's worth a try? Until we get an idea who's after us, we'll never get another quiet moment. If he thinks it's all ridiculous, I think we'll be able to tell if he's telling the truth."

"I don't really want to go."

"Then you wait here. I'll go."

"No, we may as well stick together. Do you want to go now?"

"We'll wait until this evening. We'll start watching about six o'clock."

During the rest of the afternoon, Maggie tried to talk Fell out of the idea, but his face was grim and set. He was determined to go.

To add to Maggie's fears, Dunwiddy phoned to say they were short of men and he had called off their guard.

They set out just before six. The air was hot and clammy and from far away came the distant rumble of thunder.

Maggie parked at the end of the street. "If we wait here," she said, "we can see her if she drives past." And in her heart of hearts, Maggie prayed that she would not drive past, or that if she did, she would have the inspector in the passenger seat and then they could go home and she would have time to talk Fell out of this crazy idea.

Seven o'clock came and went. Then eight. Maggie began to relax. The thunder crashed overhead and fat raindrops began to splash on the windscreen. Maggie switched on the wipers. By the time nine o'clock shone greenly from the clock on the dashboard, Maggie opened her mouth to suggest they should go home, but Fell suddenly hissed, "Car coming."

They both crouched down and peered over the dashboard. A grey Mercedes passed them. Despite the pouring rain, they could briefly make out Gloria Lewis behind the wheel.

"Let's go," said Fell.

Maggie drove forward and parked opposite the inspector's villa. "I haven't an umbrella."

"Come on," said Fell. "A little bit of rain never hurt anyone."

Maggie switched off the engine and got out of the car, gasping as the rain struck down on her. Lightning lit up the front of the villa. Thunder rolled and crashed overhead. They both ran up the drive to the front door. Fell, water running down his face, rang the bell.

They waited. He rang again. Again they waited.

"Well, that's that," said Maggie. "Let's go."

"We'll walk round the side of the house and see if there's a light on," said Fell. "He may not be answering the door."

Maggie groaned inwardly. But she followed Fell through the shrubbery and round the side of the house. "Look," hissed Fell, clutching her arm. Light was streaming out from a window at the back of the garden.

They walked up to the window. Inspector Rudfern was sitting watching television.

Fell rapped on the French window. The inspector heaved himself to his feet.

"The gun," whispered Maggie urgently. "What if he's got Andy Briggs's gun?"

Rudfern opened the window. "Who's out there?"

"Fell Dolphin."

"I might have known. Come in."

Fell and Maggie walked inside. The inspector tugged at a cord and a venetian blind dropped down to hide the window. Then he locked it.

"Sit down," he said.

"We're a bit wet." Fell looked anxiously towards the now closed window. A huge crack of thunder reverberated through the room.

Rudfern said nothing, merely sitting down again.

Maggie and Fell sat down opposite him. Maggie could feel her wet clothes sticking to her. Droplets of rainwater were running down her face.

"Well?" prompted Rudfern.

Fell opened his mouth to say weakly that they had just dropped by to talk about the train robbery but found himself blurting out, "We think you did it."

Rudfern looked wearily at him. "And what gives you that idea?"

Fell took a deep breath. "It's all wild guessing. But your daughter was seen wearing a Versace dress. How could she afford it? Secondly, the police think there was Semtex put in our car engine in an attempt to blow us up. There was a raid on some IRA members ten years ago, and among other things a quantity of Semtex was seized. You would have been in an ideal position to take some."

Rudfern looked at him quizzically. "And that's it?"

"Yes, but all the same—"

"Have you talked to Dunwiddy about this?"

"No, but we're going to."

He studied them for some minutes and then unexpectedly quoted King Lear. "Sharper than a serpent's tooth it is to have a thankless child."

Silence.

Maggie wanted to say, "We'd better be going, then." Somewhere out there was a safe and normal world and she wanted to return to it.

But Rudfern suddenly started speaking again. "I had planned to wait a couple or more years and then leave the country. Get a nice villa somewhere sunny with a view of the sea, but she couldn't wait."

"Gloria? Your daughter?" asked Fell.

"Who else? She'd married a rich man and the marriage had come unstuck. But she'd had a taste of high living and she wanted it back. I loved her. My wife had died and she was all I had. I would have given her the world. But I'd always been an honest copper and had no intention of changing when I got the news that a trainload of currency was going to be passing through Buss. I got a bit tight one evening at the Rotary club and told this Colonel Wakeham all about it."

"You said a military man had planned it all," said Fell miserably. "So the colonel was a crook."

"That old buffer? No. But he liked crosswords and detective stories and so he began, as a joke, to map out the perfect robbery. He wrote down copious notes and gave them to me.

"I still didn't think about doing anything about it when Tarry Briggs was brought in for questioning over an armed robbery at a building society in the High Street. I lied and said I had proof that he'd done it. He said he wanted to do a deal and would only talk to me. I switched off the tape recorder and then I was alone in the interview room with him. I thought he was going to give me a tip-off of some other burglaries or put his hands up to more and do a deal that way, but it turned out he knew about the Post Office money. He said it could be taken easily. He said he could recruit three others. If I took part, I would get the lion's share."

"He must have known you could be corrupted," said Fell.

"No, he didn't. He was desperate not to go to prison again.

But I had the colonel's plan. And who would ever suspect me? But I still felt I couldn't do it. I said he was mad and left him. He was being held in the cells overnight. Unfortunately, I went home to Gloria and Gloria had found the colonel's robbery plan in my suit pocket."

The thunder rumbled, but farther away now.

"She went on all night about how this was our chance. I owed it to her. I would be in charge of the investigation. Nothing could go wrong. I pointed out that with such a sum stolen, Scotland Yard would become involved. She shrugged and said as long as I made sure no clues were left and the robbery took place quickly and efficiently, then we had nothing to worry about."

"But didn't my . . . I mean didn't the colonel guess you had been behind it? That is if it followed his plan."

"Silly old man. Afterwards, he kept shaking his head and saying, 'Bless my soul. What a coincidence.' Never suspected me for a minute. Remember, I was in charge of the investigation. I saw that the charges against Tarry Briggs were dropped. He grinned and said he'd get the others together. He got Johnny Tremp for a start."

Fell could not restrain himself. "Johnny Tremp! But we were told he had won the lottery."

"He never had much in the way of brains," said Rudfern. "He figured out if he gave the local paper the story of his supposed win, he could begin to spend. I said, why the hell didn't he get out of the country, but he said he'd never been out of England and didn't intend to start now."

"But the lottery people must have seen the story and realized he was lying," said Maggie.

"No, it was only in the local paper and they missed it. That surprised me. I was sure they would have a cuttings agency and that someone would spot it, but with so many lottery winners twice a week, it went unnoticed."

"And the others?" asked Fell.

"Myself. It was part of the deal that I should put on a mask and take part. Then there were two local villains, Snotty Duggan and Harry Finn. When I started the planning, I realized it was simple, just like a police operation. Then that fool, Tarry, had to lose his cool and beat that guard to death. Snotty and Harry, along with every local villain, were pulled in for questioning, but we had all fixed up alibis.

"Snotty and Harry disappeared, God knows where. Tarry legged it to Spain, but fortunately for me, at that time we had no extradition treaty with Spain and by the time we did, he was dead.

"That brings me to your father."

"What about him?" asked Fell.

"He kept calling round at the police station and making a nuisance of himself. He said his name had been blackened. I told Gloria I was sure he suspected me, but she had become as hard as iron. She had turned into a monster. She wanted to begin digging into the money as soon as possible.

"I forced her to wait until I was retired and warned her to go carefully."

"Andy Briggs, Tarry Briggs's son, the one that was killed," said Fell. "He called on us, saying he knew that my father had been part of the robbery."

"He came here first," said Rudfern. "Gloria told me to get rid of him until she thought what to do. He thought Dolphin had been in on the robbery. I didn't correct him. He was ranting and raving and making accusations all over the palce. I said to give me a day to work things out. God, what a relief when the bastard was murdered. Then you pair started poking your noses in and Gloria freaked. She remembered Dolphin had suspected something. I think she had become unhinged. When I read of the burglary on your place, I taxed her with it, and she said she had masqueraded as a postman and broken in and searched your place to see if you had anything hidden away."

Maggie hugged her wet body and shivered, remembering the slashed furniture. It had been the work of an insane woman.

"She began to say we had to get rid of you."

"So you did have some of that Semtex from the raid?" said Fell.

"No, I had no reason to take it. Gloria went to Johnny Tremp. He said he would fix it. He had the criminal connections, and if you've got the money, you can get your hands on anything in this country. When that attempt failed, Johnny threatened Gloria. He said she was overreacting. She was to shut up and sit quiet."

"Someone pushed me in the river and tried to drown me," said Fell. "Was that your daughter?"

"I don't know, I can't see why. Can you swim?"

"No."

"Well, she wouldn't know that. Probably some drunk or some of the jolly youth of Buss zonked out on Ecstasy pills."

Fell then asked the question Maggie dreaded. "Why are you telling us all this now?"

Rudfern relapsed into silence. Maggie wondered if she could dash to the window and unlock it.

Then he said, half to himself, "I had good days in the police force. I had a good record. I liked the camaraderie. But after the robbery, there was only Gloria, getting more and more unhinged. And down at the station, well, I knew there were mutters that I hadn't worked hard enough on the case. I retired. I bought this house. I began to become increasingly frightened of Gloria. What a silly, stupid thing to have done. I haven't had a day's peace since the robbery."

Fell got up very slowly and walked to the window. He gently raised the blind and then unlocked the French window. He held out his hand to Maggie. "Come along."

She scrambled to join him. He put an arm around her.

"We'll need to take this to Dunwiddy," said Fell.

Rudfern looked at them, his eyes old and sad. "Do what you have to. I'm sick of the whole thing."

The rain outside was coming down in sheets. Hand in hand, Maggie and Fell ran round the side of the house. Fell suddenly seized Maggie and drew her back into the shrubbery.

"Gloria," whispered Fell.

They waited until they saw Gloria Lewis get out of her car, unfurl an umbrella and hurry to the house. They waited, huddled together, until they heard her go in and shut the door behind her.

"Now!" hissed Fell. "Let's run for it!"

They darted across to the car. Maggie unlocked it and they got in. "Let's go home first and dry out and then we'll contact Dunwiddy," said Fell.

Maggie drove off with a hideous grinding of gears. "I'm so frightened," she said, "I've practically forgotten how to drive."

"Just get us home." Fell shivered. "I was terrified he was going to shoot us."

Once safely inside their home, they went upstairs. Maggie

took out two large bath-sheets. "We'd better get dried and changed and go straight to the police station."

Fell went into his room and stripped off. He rubbed himself down briskly and then put on clean clothes.

"Ready, Maggie?" he called.

No reply.

He went into her room. She was sitting on the edge of her bed, naked. She was shaking and tears were rolling down her face.

"Oh, Maggie," said Fell, sitting down beside her and gathering her in his arms. "It's all over. We'll go to the police, and . . . oh, please don't cry."

He kissed her eyes and then he kissed her lips. It was a warm and comforting sensation, so he kissed her again . . . and again. The surge of passion that shook him was electrifying. He was suddenly aware of her naked body, of the weight of her breasts against his chest.

"Why, Maggie," he said, his voice full of wonder. "Maggie!"

She gave a choked little sob and collapsed back onto the bed, pulling him on top of her. Her eyes without the shield of her heavy glasses looked wide and vulnerable.

After ten minutes of rising passion and kissing and caressing, Fell whispered, "Maggie, I've never before. I mean, I'm . . ."

"I know," said Maggie. "Take your clothes off and come to me."

Fell awoke, a smile on his lips. His arm under Maggie's body was getting cramped. He eased it out and then he realized it was daylight outside and that they had both fallen asleep after more passionate lovemaking than he had ever even dreamt of.

"Maggie," he said, "wake up. The police. We've got to go to the police!"

Maggie blinked, then she was suddenly full awake. "Oh, Fell, what are they going to say to us? How on earth are we going to explain why we didn't go to them immediately? Rudfern and Gloria will have fled."

Fell looked at the clock beside the bed. "It's only six o'clock. We could lie and say we went to see Rudfern in the middle of the night."

"Maybe we'll just tell them we were too frightened to approach them in case they wouldn't believe us," said Maggie.

"We'll try that. But we've got to go."

Maggie wound her arms around him and kissed him, and his reaction was so passionate that it was another twenty minutes before they both crawled groggily out of bed.

After they were dressed and were hurrying down the stairs, Fell stopped abruptly and swung round. "Is it all right—about last night, I mean?"

"Oh, yes, *yes*."

They stared at each other for a long moment, two ordinary people made in a brief moment extraordinary by the force of their love for each other.

They set the burglar alarm and went outside. It was a cool, windy day with great puffy clouds sailing across a blue sky.

At the police station, they were told that it was Inspector Dunwiddy's day off. But when Fell started saying that he knew who had committed the train robbery and that the thieves might even now be getting away, the desk sergeant had them put into an interviewing room and phoned Dunwiddy.

When the inspector arrived, Fell told him rapidly everything they had found out from Rudfern. When he had finished, Dunwiddy said, "You pair wait right here. I'll need a statement from you and I'll need you to explain why you delayed coming here to tell me this."

An hour dragged past. The day outside darkened and rain patterned against the window of the interviewing room.

At last Fell said, "I'm cold and this is ridiculous. Let's go home. We can have a meal and be comfortable and wait for Dunwiddy there."

"I think they might try to stop us going," said Maggie.

"We'll see." He took Maggie's hand and they walked out of the interviewing room and down a long corridor. When they got to the door leading out to the front area, Fell pressed the buzzer to release the door lock and they walked through.

"Where are you going?" demanded the desk sergeant.

"We'll be at home," said Fell. "Inspector Dunwiddy can find us there."

"You were told to wait here."

"We haven't been charged and we're not running away," said Fell calmly. "You know where to find us."

The phone on the desk rang before the sergeant could say anything further and so they just walked out.

"He'll be so angry," moaned Maggie.

"He's angry with us anyway," commented Fell airily. He stretched his arms up to the rainy sky and laughed. "I feel marvellous. Look at it this way. If it hadn't been for us, he wouldn't have found out anything at all."

"Let's hope he feels that way," said Maggie, unlocking the car.

†

But they grew increasingly nervous as the day dragged on with no sign of Dunwiddy. All Fell wanted to do was to take Maggie upstairs and make love to her again.

It was evening before the doorbell rang, making them both jump. A policeman and a policewoman stood on the step. "You're to come with us to the station," said the policeman.

He waited while they both got their coats, coats they had not worn all that dandelion summer. In the car, Fell asked, "What's been going on?"

"The inspector will tell you," said the policeman.

Maggie and Fell were ushered back into the interviewing room. They sat huddled in their coats. "You need a new coat," said Fell, eyeing the shabby black number Maggie was wearing.

The door opened and Dunwiddy came in, followed by a detective and a policewoman. The policewoman put a tape in a machine on the wall, and Dunwiddy sat down and said, "Interview with Mr. Fellworth Dolphin and Miss Margaret Partlett beginning at"—he looked at his watch—"twenty-one hours fifty."

Fell and Maggie sat down opposite Dunwiddy, who was flanked by his detective. The policewoman took a chair in the corner.

"Now," said Dunwiddy, "begin at the beginning again."

And so Fell did, repeating everything that Rudfern had told him, except for the bit about Andy Briggs.

When he had finished, Dunwiddy said, "Now will you explain why you delayed until early this morning to let us know this?"

"We were afraid," lied Fell. "Rudfern was one of you. We

had no real proof. We sat up all night wondering what to do. Look at it from our point of view. It was his word against ours."

"You're forgetting about Johnny Tremp. We pulled him in. We checked with the lottery people. He never won anything. He thought Gloria Lewis had shopped him and so he told us the lot. Rudfern is dead."

"What!" exclaimed Maggie and Fell in unison.

"It appears that he shot himself with an old service revolver. We're still investigating that in case his daughter shot him and made it look like suicide, but we're pretty sure it is. He left a note saying he was sick of the whole thing. That's all he said. 'I'm sick of the whole thing.' "

Maggie took Fell's hand in her own. She had turned quite white. An old service revolver could mean that the inspector shot himself with Andy Briggs's gun, and if he had, then her fingerprints and Fell's would be on it.

In a quavering voice, she said, "Your forensic men will find more than one set of fingerprints on it if his daughter shot him."

Dunwiddy sighed. "A preliminary investigation shows there is only one set of prints on that gun."

Colour flooded Maggie's face.

"And where is Gloria Lewis?" she asked.

"Gone, thanks to you pair. We're watching all the ports and airports. You could have charges laid against you for impeding the police in their inquiries."

"What!" demanded Fell wrathfully. "You do that and we'll go to the press about how it was us, on our own, who solved your case."

"Are you threatening me?" roared Dunwiddy.

"Why not?" demanded Fell. "You were threatening us."

"We'll discuss this later," said the inspector. "You will wait here until your statements are typed up. Then you will both sign them and hold yourself in readiness for further questioning. You are not to leave Buss."

"Was any of the money recovered?" asked Fell.

"We found a lot of it in Johnny Tremp's house. Of course, over the years, he had changed the notes. We also found a small quantity of Semtex."

"What about Rudfern's house?"

"Nothing there. If there ever was anything, then Gloria Lewis took it with her."

Dunwiddy terminated the interview. Fell and Maggie were left alone. "Don't say anything," Fell whispered. "They might be listening."

"Fell . . . ," began Maggie.

"What?"

She looked down and muttered, "Nothing."

Fell studied her for a few moments, a smile curving his lips as he remembered the night before. Then he realized that even in the height of his passion, he had never mentioned love.

He looked around the dingy interviewing room. Then he pushed back his chair and got down on one knee.

He took Maggie's hand in his. "Margaret Partlett," he said. "I love you and want to marry you as soon as possible. What do you say?"

Maggie's face as she looked at him seemed to be lit up from within. "Oh, yes," she said. "I think I've loved you from the first moment I saw you."

Fell stood up and held out his arms. Maggie rose and went into them.

The door opened and a policewoman bearing a tray with tea and biscuits stood for a moment watching the passionately embracing couple. Then she withdrew, still carrying the tray, and quietly closed the door behind her.

In the following days, Fell and Maggie, insulated to a certain extent by love, waited anxiously for news that Gloria Lewis had been found. What if the madwoman came back to exact revenge?

Gloria's photograph was shown in all the newspapers and on television. Dunwiddy called on them and said he was confident that she would soon be picked up. He was almost fatherly towards them, for neither Fell nor Maggie had claimed any credit for solving the mystery of the train robbery and Dunwiddy was basking in national fame.

Autumn had arrived and the heat of the dandelion summer was only a memory as days of steady rain drummed down.

Fell and Maggie began to plan their wedding day. Maggie wanted to get married in church, although Fell would have preferred a simple ceremony in a registry office. But Maggie felt that being on that bridge just at the time that Fell was in the river had been no coincidence.

Gradually the old living room was being transformed into the country kitchen that Fell wanted. It was after he had spent what he considered a small fortune on a very beautiful antique Welsh dresser that he confided to Maggie that they really should think of going into business after they were married.

Maggie was still very keen on the idea of a bookshop and Fell finally decided it was a good plan. They travelled around, consulting booksellers, reading up on bookshop management, and at last renting a shop in the High Street not far from Melissa's health shop.

The wedding date was set for the first week in October at

St. Peter's. Fell had engaged the services of an organist. Maggie had pleaded with him to invite his "relatives" and also suggested he should invite old Mrs. Wakeham. It took some persuasion because Fell was still bitter about the circumstances of his birth, but he wanted the wedding to be special for Maggie, so he at last gave in to her requests.

Now they bought all the newspapers and watched television news, hoping to hear that Gloria had been found. Maggie longed to have all the ends tied up before the wedding. Then there were the other two men who had also taken part in the robbery. Rudfern hadn't known where they were, but surely they would not dare come back to Buss. Interpol was looking for the couple as well as for Gloria.

Then, a week before the wedding, Dunwiddy called. "Good news," he said.

Maggie's eyes shone with relief. "You've got Gloria!"

"No, not her. But we found out about the other two, Snotty Duggan and Harry Finn. Snotty—real name, George—and Harry are both dead. They moved to Turkey, to the south coast, and then had this idea of getting into the drugs racket to increase their wealth. The local mafia are not fond of interlopers and so the pair of them were murdered, and only two years ago. I had never come across them in their villainous days here, and although their murders got a small paragraph in the newspaper, it didn't mean anything to me. Rudfern must have known; God knows why he would lie."

"Maybe it was a news item that passed him by," said Fell. "I think he would have told us otherwise. I mean, he told us everything else."

"From what we've gathered," said Dunwiddy, "Rudfern had begun to hate his own daughter. Their cleaning woman said they were constantly quarrelling and having scenes. She now tells us she overheard Rudfern saying, 'I'll shop you,' and Gloria replying, 'You can't. I'll bring you down with me.' "

Maggie shivered. "I don't like to think of her out there."

"Don't worry," said the inspector. "There's one place in the world she won't dare show her face and that's Buss!"

EPILOGUE

†

MAGGIE and Fell had decided to spend their honeymoon in Paris and then begin work on the bookshop as soon as they got back.

Fell had asked his "cousin" Tom to be best man. He had finally agreed with Maggie that to have some pretend relatives was better than having none at all. Mrs. Moule, complete with Zimmer frame, was to be Maggie's maid of honour. Maggie had invited her mother and could only hope that she would not get drunk at the reception, which was to be held at the Palace Hotel.

Maggie studied her wedding outfit. It was a green silk suit. She had been watching her diet so that there would be no danger of it straining at the seams when she went to the church in the morning.

As she came down from the bedroom, she heard the doorbell ring. Fell was out in the garden. He called, "Will you get that, Maggie?"

Fell had put his "relatives" up at the Palace Hotel, but Maggie thought one of them might be calling round. And so it turned out. Aunt Agnes stood on the step. "I thought I'd bring your wedding present round," she said. "You'll want to take it on your honeymoon."

"Come in," said Maggie as Fell came in from the garden. "Aunt Agnes has brought us a present," said Maggie.

"What on earth have you done here?" demanded Aunt Agnes, looking round at the new kitchen. "What on earth do you need a big kitchen like this for?"

Fell sighed. "It suits us."

"It looks odd to me."

"Mind if we open your present?" Fell wanted to stop any more criticism.

He unwrapped the paper. Revealed were two pink hot-water bottles in the shape of fuzzy teddy bears.

"How sweet," said Maggie quickly, as a look of horror crossed Fell's face.

"It'll be a hard winter, mark my words," said Aunt Agnes, "and you'll need to keep warm on your honeymoon."

Maggie began to giggle helplessly. "I don't see what's so funny," said Aunt Agnes, bridling. "I took my hot-water bottle on my honeymoon and I was glad of it."

Fell began to laugh as well and then Maggie said in a choked voice, "That's the doorbell. I'll get it."

Still laughing, she opened the door. A thin man stood there, a baseball cap pulled down over his eyes. "Come to read the meter," he said.

"Could I see some identification?" asked Maggie.

He thrust his hand into his pocket and pulled out a small pistol. "Get inside," he ordered.

White-faced, Maggie backed into the house.

The "man" dragged his baseball cap off his head, revealing the hard features and glittering eyes of Gloria Lewis.

In the kitchen, Fell and Aunt Agnes stared, astonished.

"You!" said Fell. He made a move towards the phone.

"Stay where you are," snarled Gloria.

"What do you want?" demanded Fell.

"I want you dead, you interfering bastard. My father would be alive today if it weren't for you. I'm tired of running."

"Look," said Fell. "The police only want you as an accessory to the robbery. You kill me and it's murder. As it stands at the moment, a good lawyer could get you off."

"No, he couldn't. This is Britain, and you get a longer jail sentence for robbery than you do for murder. You're for it."

Her eyes glittered madly, but the hand holding the gun never wavered.

"Ho, just you wait a minute," cried Aunt Agnes. "Nobody's going to shoot my nephew."

A small figure in a tightly buttoned-up tweed coat, she placed herself in front of Fell.

"Get out of the way!" raged Gloria.

"Auntie, do as she says," ordered Fell.

"No," said Aunt Agnes. "Guns don't frighten me. She's nothing but a bully."

And Gloria shot her.

Maggie, who had edged around behind Gloria, screamed and threw herself on her, love and terror lending her mad strength.

Fell, who had never hit anyone in his life before, drew back his fist and struck Gloria full on the chin. Her head rocked back and she slumped in Maggie's arms.

The gun rattled to the floor.

"Tie her up," said Maggie. "Aunt Agnes. Is she still alive?"

Fell knelt down. "I don't know," he said. "I'll phone an ambulance. And the police. There's string in that drawer there, Maggie. Can you tie Gloria up?"

Maggie nodded. While Fell phoned, she fumbled with the string, her hands shaking so much she thought she would never be able to get Gloria's hands and ankles tied. But at last she achieved it and then rushed upstairs to the bathroom and was violently sick.

Fell slumped down on the floor beside the body of his "aunt" and nursed his swollen and bleeding knuckles. The day suddenly seemed unnaturally quiet.

And then he could hear the sound of sirens.

Maggie crept down the stairs as the first cars drew up outside the house.

Then the kitchen was full of police, followed by ambulance men. The paramedics said that Aunt Agnes was still alive . . . just. Gloria was lifted up and taken off.

Dunwiddy arrived and the questioning began. After a time, Fell cut him off. "We're both shocked and I have to get to the hospital to see my aunt. You know where to find us. For God's sake, give us a little peace."

"All right, but I'll be back. That was some knock-out punch you gave her."

Fell looked down at his swollen and bleeding knuckles. "It never hurts in books," he said.

At last Maggie and Fell were left alone. "We'll need to cancel the wedding," said Maggie wearily.

"Oh, God, what a mess," mourned Fell. "All I want to do is go to bed and sleep for a week."

"You go to the hospital, I'll cancel all the arrangements and guests, and then I'll follow you there. I'll phone and get you a cab."

The doorbell rang. "Now what?" asked Fell. "Someone else come to kill us?"

Maggie gave a shaky laugh. "There's nobody left." She answered the door. It was Peter with his photographer, Derek.

"What's going on, Maggie?" he asked. "Someone tipped us off that the place was full of police."

"We haven't any time to speak to you now," said Fell, appearing behind Maggie.

"It's all right," said Maggie. "Have you got a mobile phone?"

"Yes," said Peter.

"Then come in. I'll tell you what happened and then you can help me to cancel all the wedding arrangements."

And so Peter got the story that was to land him a plum job on one of the national newspapers.

When Maggie finally arrived at the hospital, it was to find Fell sitting in the reception area. "She's going to live, Maggie," he said. "The bullet went through the side of her body. They say she'll live. Whoever would have thought she would be so brave?"

"She saved our lives." Maggie sat down next to him. "Peter helped me cancel all the wedding arrangements."

"I'll bet he enjoyed that."

"Well, he did, rather."

A doctor approached them. "Mr. Dolphin?"

"Yes, my aunt . . . ?"

"She's resting comfortably. She's lost a lot of blood but she is going to be all right. There is no need for you to wait. You'll be able to see her tomorrow."

Maggie drove Fell home. He stood looking around the kitchen. "Do you think we want to go on staying here, Maggie? So many bad memories."

Maggie walked to the stairs and turned and held out her hand. "There are good ones as well."

Fell looked at her. Her face was white and her eyes still red with weeping. Her hair was lank. All he saw was a beautiful woman. He took her hand in his and they went up the stairs together.

It transpired that Rudfern had salted away a great deal of the robbery money in a Swiss bank. Dunwiddy had taken to dropping in on them for a chat. He said that Gloria's brain appeared to have cracked and it would be doubtful if she would ever be considered sane enough to stand trial. He was delighted to be asked to their wedding, which had been rescheduled.

Fell was looking forward to their honeymoon, to get peace and quiet, and above all, to get away from Aunt Agnes who, fully recovered, was as carping and irritating as ever. She, too, had become a frequent visitor, and how, thought Fell, can you send someone away who has saved your life?

At last the day of their wedding arrived, a cold, brisk, bright day, with the last of the red and gold leaves of autumn fluttering down from the trees in the churchyard of St. Peter's Church.

Maggie and Fell were still local celebrities, and so the church was full of sightseers as well as Fell's "relatives." Maggie's mother was there in an acid pink suit and a huge pink hat. Mrs. Moule, very excited at being maid of honour, had her Zimmer frame decorated with paper roses. Cousin Tom acted as Fell's best man. Maggie was given away by Inspector Dunwiddy, who looked as large and untidy as ever in a morning suit which he had obviously not worn in years because it was too tight on him.

The vicar, Mr. Sneddon, had heeded Fell's warning not to have any steel bands, and so the wedding march was played by an odd ensemble of young people with white spotty and villainous faces on two guitars, a glockenspiel, an electric keyboard, and a tambourine.

To Maggie, the day was perfect, and even when her mother got disgracefully drunk at the wedding reception at the Palace Hotel and tried to sit on the vicar's lap, she felt that nothing could ever dim her happiness.

She did feel, however, that old Mrs. Wakeham, who had failed to make an appearance, might at least have written to Fell.

They left for their honeymoon, surrounded by cheering crowds. Maggie threw her bouquet, which was caught with amazing deftness by old Mrs. Moule.

And so they went to Paris on their honeymoon, and once abroad, decided to travel on to Vienna, Prague and Budapest. They stayed at the best hotels in each city and spent a great deal of money.

It was only when they returned home after six weeks that Fell began to worry about money. There was still plenty left, but they had spent so lavishly on the new kitchen, the wedding reception and the honeymoon that he was horrified at how so much had melted away. The bookshop was a problem. Stock would have to be bought. The lease had been paid. But it would be some time before they could start making a profit. And a bookshop in Buss? Would anyone come? He wished now he had talked Maggie into starting a restaurant. There was always room for another restaurant in Buss. But he kept his worries to himself. He was so deeply in love with Maggie that he wanted to protect her from any anxiety.

One morning, after they had been back for a week, the phone rang. It was Mr. Jamieson, the lawyer. "Could you step around to my office, Mr. Dolphin?" he asked. "I have something of interest for you."

Maggie was out shopping and so Fell left her a note on the kitchen table and started walking towards the market square. Snow was beginning to fall from a steel grey sky.

What on earth did the lawyer want to see him about? Perhaps the lawyer had heard from the bank manager about his profligate ways and wanted to give him a warning.

Fell mounted the steps to the lawyer's office.

"Come in," said Mr. Jamieson expansively. "Tea?"

"No, thank you," said Fell nervously. "What's all this about?"

"Sit down. I have the papers here."

Fell sat down in a chair opposite the lawyer. He could hear the noises from the market below, just as he had heard them on the day he had learned of his inheritance.

"Do you know a Mrs. Wakeham?" asked the lawyer.

Fell wondered whether to deny any knowledge of her but settled for a cautious "I met her once."

"And that was your only connection?"

"Yes."

"Amazing. You know she is dead?"

"No," said Fell bleakly. He had nursed one last rosy dream of getting together with his grandmother at last, having one family blood tie. "When did she die?"

"Three weeks ago."

"I didn't know. I'm not long back from an extended honeymoon."

"So you did not know her very well?"

"What is this about?" snapped Fell, terrified that something had happened to reveal the secret of his birth.

"Mrs. Mary Wakeham of Fellworth Manor . . ." He stopped and looked curiously at Fell. "Of course, how silly of me. Fellworth Manor and your name is Fellworth."

Fell suddenly remembered that sunny day when he and Maggie had gone to see Mrs. Wakeham and how she had recognized Maggie's merit before he had become aware of it himself.

He said, "As a lawyer, anything I say to you must be in confidence?"

"Of course."

So Fell, relaxed by that thought of Maggie, and by the awareness that being a bastard no longer carried the stigma it would have done twenty years ago, told the lawyer the secret of his birth.

"Ah, that explains it," beamed Mr. Jamieson.

"Explains what?"

"I will let you have a copy of her will. But the long and the short of it is that after she left the house and grounds to the National Trust and various other bequests, the bulk of her fortune, which is seven hundred and fifty thousand pounds, goes to you."

There was a silence broken only by the sounds of the market. Fell stared at the lawyer. Mr. Jamieson took out a sealed envelope. "This is addressed to you, to be given to you after her death."

Fell opened it and began to read.

"Dear Fellworth," Mrs. Wakeham had written, "I have developed terminal cancer and do not expect to be alive for your wedding. You have had an unnecessarily hard life and I hope things in the future will be better for you. To facilitate this, I am leaving you a sum in my will. All my best wishes for the future. Mary Wakeham."

Fell read the short letter over and over. Then he looked up at the lawyer. "I would rather have had her alive and well and willing to see me than this money."

"Money's money," said the lawyer briskly.

"And they do throw it at you," murmured Fell, "when they can't give love."

Fell's bookshop opened on the day Melissa's health shop closed down. It was stacked with bright new books. They had a coffee shop at the back with a few tables. Maggie had baked a large supply of scones and little sponge cakes.

Curious customers wandered in. Some went through to the coffee shop. By the afternoon, the coffee shop seemed full of chattering customers. Fell heard one woman exclaim, "Ethel came in here by chance this morning and phoned me and said, 'You must try their sponge cakes. Never tasted anything so light and delicious.' "

Maggie might find out they would be better off running a café instead, thought Fell.

He sat behind the desk in the front of the shop and opened a new detective story and read the first line. "Bert Jensen, six feet of muscle, cut down his assailant with a single karate chop." Fell smiled. He felt suddenly amazingly happy. From now on life would be full of love and interest—but no adventures. All the blood and mayhem was now neatly tucked away in all the shiny covers of the books surrounding him.

But he would never forget that dandelion summer.